The Sheikh's American Daughter

Kate Goldman

The Sheikh's American Daughter

Published by Kate Goldman

ISBN 978-1-07044-269-3

First printing, 2019

www.KateGoldmanBooks.com

PRINTED IN THE UNITED STATES OF AMERICA

Dedication

I want to dedicate this book to my beloved husband, who makes every day in my life worthwhile. Thank you for believing in me when nobody else does, giving me encouragement when I need it the most, and loving me simply for being myself.

Table of Contents

Chapter 1

"What?" Olivia spat out, with eyes widened to the size of olives. Surely she had heard wrong. The shock of her mother's passing was messing with her senses. Even though her mother had been battling cancer, she could not come to terms with her death. She felt it was too soon. "Please repeat what you just said," Olivia said to her mother's lawyer, Mr. Jackson.

"The only thing I can leave you is the identity of your father. He is alive and well in Lebanon. Please go to him. My last wish is that you meet your father," Mr. Jackson read out the will. Olivia's wavy brown tresses shook as she shook her head in disbelief.

"My father?"

To her knowledge, her father had died before she was born. Twenty-three years later and after her mother's passing, she had found out that he was alive all this time. It made no sense to her at all. Her best friend Daya took Olivia's hand into hers.

"Her father died a long time ago," Daya said to Mr. Jackson.

"He is still alive." Mr. Jackson pulled a piece of paper out of the folder. "When your mother left this will for you, she also left your father's name and address." He handed Olivia the paper. She just stared at him in disbelief. Daya took the paper instead.

"Solomon Habib," Daya read out. She crossed her eyebrows. "Lebanon!" she spat out.

"What about Lebanon?" Olivia asked.

"He is from Lebanon."

"Let me see." Olivia took the paper from Daya. "Okay, let me get this straight, my father is still alive and he is Lebanese."

"Yes." Mr. Jackson nodded. He handed Olivia a white envelope.

"What's this now?" Olivia could not handle any more surprises.

"A plane ticket."

"Why should I bother going to look for him? He did not bother to look for me all this time."

"Exactly. Where has he been for all this time?" Daya interjected.

"You must be feeling confused and angry right now. However, if you do not go, you will regret it. You will still be wondering why he was never present in your life," said Mr. Jackson. He made sense but Olivia did not want to listen. She was not done mourning her mother, and then she was hit with such a surprise.

***

"Are you ready?" Daya asked Olivia as they buckled their seatbelts ready to land in Lebanon. She was accompanying her to Lebanon. The two of them had been inseparable since they were five years old. So of course Daya was going with Olivia.

"I wish my mother had told me about him when she was alive. Why did she have to wait until she was dead?" Olivia was full of mixed emotions. She was still grieving over her mother, and she was angry about her father. Where had he been when her mother worked two jobs to support them? Where had he been when she had to take a part-time job at the age of fifteen to help her mother out? She needed him to answer those questions.

"I guess we are going to get your answers pretty soon," Daya replied.

After the plane had landed smoothly, the passengers took their hand luggage and exited the plane. They went into the airport to collect the rest of their luggage. Olivia felt as though they waited for their luggage for too long. She was a little impatient. She looked around as she waited. Foreigners exited the airport; some Middle Eastern men dressed in expensive suits walked past her. It made her wonder about her father's identity.

After getting their luggage, Olivia and Daya went to look for a taxi. She fished the address out of her pocket and showed it to the driver. "We want to go here," she said to him. The older grey-haired man looked at the address and then nodded. He put their luggage into the trunk of the car.

"Are you here to visit?" he asked.

"Yes," Olivia replied as she got into the car.

"Have you ever been here before?"

"No."

"It is very nice here." He started the engine.

"And very hot it seems," Daya replied. Olivia just sank into the backseat and stared out of the window. The city looked nice indeed. It was a shame that she was not there to enjoy the country.

They finally arrived at their destination after what seemed like forever. Olivia paid the driver before she hopped out of the car. "Maybe we should have checked into a hotel first," Olivia said to Daya.

"Maybe." Daya laughed a little. They walked towards the security guards standing outside the tall gates.

"Excuse me, we are looking for Solomon Habib," Olivia said to them. They looked at each other and then back at her.

"Who are you?" one of the security guards said to her.

"Olivia."

"Appointment?"

"No, we do not have an appointment."

"Then you cannot come in."

Daya frowned. "Why not?" she asked him. Just then, an expensive Bentley pulled up. The window rolled down and a man sitting in the backseat asked the security guard something in Arabic. The security guard responded in Arabic.

"What business do you have with the sheikh?" the gentleman in the car asked.

"Sheikh?" Daya and Olivia said at the same time. They looked at each other in shock.

"I heard that he was my father. So I need to speak to him," Olivia replied. The dark-skinned, handsome gentleman in the car raised his dark eyebrows.

"That's ludicrous," said the man.

"I think so too but I need to speak with him in order to find out the truth."

The man did not say anything for a moment. He just looked at Olivia from head to toe. He said something to the security guards in Arabic and then rolled up his window. He drove into the compound.

"He says you may enter," the security guard said to them. "But leave your bags here."

"Fine," Olivia agreed. It wasn't like she was planning to stay anyway. They walked into the compound and headed up to the large house. The house had grey stone walls and cream windowsills. There were large brown double doors in the middle.

"This place is magnificent," said Daya as she eyed the neatly cut green lawn and the tall palm trees.

"Tell me about it." Olivia stopped walking and placed her hands on her hips. "But this guy, couldn't he give us a lift to the house or walk with us?"

The man that had stopped at the gate was standing at the front of the house, leaning against his car.

"He is clearly waiting for us. He should have given us a lift. It's a long walk from the gate," said Daya.

"Tell me about it." Olivia started walking again.

"Goodness, you walk so slow," the man from the Bentley said to Olivia and Daya when they reached the house.

"You could have given us a lift, you know," said Olivia.

"Why would I do that?" He slipped his hands in his pockets. "Let me go speak to the sheikh and see if he knows anything about this atrocity."

"Can't I just go in and speak to him myself? I just flew all the way from Atlanta, and I am not going to leave until I have spoken to him," said Olivia.

"Not just anyone can enter the house."

"Then can you call him?"

"The sheikh can't come out just because you summoned him."

"The two of you have the same eyebrows," Daya pointed out. Olivia looked at her with a frown on her face. If she was trying to be funny, this surely wasn't the time for it.

"Daya?" Olivia questioned.

"Sorry, I just noticed."

The man just shook his head. "There's the sheikh now actually," he said and gestured towards the tall older man walking out of the house with an elegant-looking woman next to him. Daya gasped.

"It's him!" she whispered. Olivia started feeling nervous.

"Jacob, is everything okay?" the sheikh asked the man from the Bentley.

"Father, there is someone here to see you," Jacob replied.

Daya gasped again. "I knew he was your brother," she whispered.

"Shh," Olivia hushed Daya.

"Without an appointment?" the sheikh asked.

"She says that she is your daughter," Jacob said and pointed at Olivia. The sheikh raised his dark eyebrows and looked at Olivia.

"My daughter?" He laughed sarcastically. "That's ridiculous."

"That's what I said."

"My God, she looks just like her," said the woman next to the sheikh, with a face as pale as a ghost.

"Mum, are you okay?" Jacob asked her.

"She looks like who?" the sheikh asked his wife.

Chapter 2

The sheikh's wife stood there pale-faced. She stared at Olivia as though as she was a ghost. She was tall and elegantly dressed. Her black hair was pinned up neatly. She had an unfriendly face. It made Olivia feel uncomfortable.

"Daaliyah, she looks like who?" the sheikh asked as he gently touched her arm.

"Elizabeth," she answered quietly. The sheikh's hazel eyes opened wide. He whipped his head in Olivia's direction and stared at her in shock.

"You know my mother?" Olivia asked the sheikh's wife.

"You are Elizabeth's daughter?" the sheikh asked her. He looked at Olivia slowly from head to toe.

"Yes. I guess you know my mother." Olivia started feeling strange. She had come all this way to find her father but she suddenly wanted to run away. The sheikh and his wife both knew her mother. The sheikh's wife knew her mother by her first name and well enough to see her features in Olivia.

"This is weird," Jacob mumbled.

"Please come in, so we can talk," Sheikh Solomon said to Olivia.

"We have somewhere to be," said Daaliyah.

"You can go ahead without me."

"No, I will just phone them." Daaliyah looked as though she did not want to miss out on that talk. Sheikh Solomon turned on his heel and headed into the house. Olivia and Daya followed him in. They both gasped when they saw the interior.

There were brown double doors straight ahead. They were open and led outside. Olivia could see the lawn and some flowers. She assumed that it was a garden. The floors were white and clean. There was a wide staircase to the left of the entrance, and to the right, there were more brown double doors leading to another room. The sheikh was walking towards it.

They followed Sheikh Solomon through the brown double doors into a large sitting room. He gestured for them to sit down in the expensive chairs. A maid rushed in. "Shall I get you anything?" she asked Sheikh Solomon.

"Some tea." He looked at Olivia. "Is tea okay?" he asked her.

"Tea is fine," Olivia answered, although she did not like tea. The maid nodded and rushed out. Olivia and Daya sat opposite Sheikh Solomon. Daaliyah and Jacob walked in and joined them at the sitting area.

Sheikh Solomon stared at Olivia for a while. He did not say anything. He just looked at her. He studied her silently. It made Olivia feel uncomfortable. Daya could not stop fidgeting. She kept looking at around and shifting in her seat.

The maid reappeared with a tray. She placed the tray on the table and poured out the tea into the cups. She quickly walked out when she was finished. Olivia sighed. She did not like the silence. It was too uncomfortable. She squared her shoulders.

"My name is Olivia Grant. I am Elizabeth's daughter." She paused for a second. Everyone in the room was staring at her as she spoke. Sheikh Solomon looked confused and in shock. Jacob looked curious. Daaliyah looked nervous, which was unsettling. "My mother passed away and left me your address," Olivia finished off.

"What?" Sheikh Solomon spat out. "Elizabeth is dead?" he asked. His face immediately went pale.

"Yes," Olivia replied.

"How?" His right hand started shaking.

"Cancer." Olivia took a deep breath. "I don't want to talk about it." She was still grieving. She did not want to talk about her mother's last few months.

"Oh God." Sheikh Solomon touched his right hand and tried to stop it from shaking but it was useless. Both his hands started shaking.

"She left me your address and said that I should come to find you. Apparently you are my father," she said. Sheikh Solomon barely reacted. He had been paralyzed with the news of her mother's death.

"Father, are you okay?" Jacob asked as he touched Sheikh Solomon's arm.

"That is not possible. You cannot be my husband's daughter," said Daaliyah.

"Aunt Lizzy had no reason to lie," said Daya. The sheikh rose to his feet.

"Excuse me," he said and stalked to the exit. Olivia and Daya looked at each other.

"Is he just going to leave in the middle of the conversation?" Olivia said to Daya.

"He's not taking the news well," she replied.

"If he cared about my mother so much, then why did he leave her to raise me all by herself?" She felt frustrated. She had come thinking that she was going to vent at him about neglecting his fatherly duties. However, none of that had gone to plan.

Daaliyah rose to her feet and walked out of the room. Jacob was still sitting down. He seemed like he did not know what to do. "This is awkward," he said. He picked up his cup of tea and took a sip. All the other cups were still on the tray.

"It's really awkward. I think coming here was a mistake," said Olivia. A maid walked into the room.

"Sheikh Solomon has asked me to come show you to your rooms," she said.

"Show who?" Daya asked.

"The two of you."

"I don't think I want to stay," said Olivia.

"You haven't gotten a proper chance to speak to him yet. You can't just leave," Daya said to her.

"We can stay in a hotel."

"He already had your luggage brought in," said the maid. "If you could please follow me."

"You came from America, right?" Jacob asked. Olivia nodded. "Long trip, you might as well stay here a night and get everything sorted before you return."

Daya stood up. "Let's at least see the room," she said. Olivia stood up. The two of them followed the maid out of the room. They headed up the staircase. When they reached the landing, they turned left and headed down the hallway.

When they reached the end of the hallway, there was a sitting area. There were sofas and a bookshelf. "That is a guest room." The maid pointed at one of several doors. "And that is also a guest room." She pointed at another door.

"I'm going to have a look at my room for the night," said Daya. She headed to the room on the left. Olivia sighed and headed to the other room. She opened the door and walked in.

The room was big, bigger than her bedroom at her small apartment in Atlanta. There was a four-poster bed positioned in the middle of the room. It was big enough to fit four people. The room had high ceilings and large windows that overlooked the driveway. The room looked like a hotel room. It was beautiful.

There was a knock on the door. Olivia went to open the door to see who it was. There was a maid standing there with her suitcase. "Thank you," Olivia said to her. She took the suitcase and put it by the door. She figured that she was not going to unpack because she was not going to be there long. She had only packed clothes for one week. She hadn't really thought anything through. She was not sure how long she wanted to stay or how long she was supposed to stay.

Olivia went to Daya's room. "Daya!" she called out as she walked in.

"This bedroom is beautiful," Daya replied.

"So we are just supposed to wait until Sheikh Solomon is ready to speak to me?"

"Do you think he is crying? He looked like he was going to cry." Daya crossed her eyebrows. "I think he really is your father and he really cared about aunt Lizzy," she added.

Olivia placed her hands on her hips. "He didn't care enough for me."

"What about his wife? Her reaction was interesting."

"Tell me about it. She went pale in the face when she saw me." Olivia ran her hand through her long, wavy hair. She was feeling anxious. She just wanted to get her answers and get out of there.

"Do you know what I realized?" Daya asked her.

"What?" Olivia replied.

"You, Jacob and Sheikh Solomon all have hazel eyes."

Olivia narrowed her gaze at Daya. "Hazel eyes are not uncommon," she said.

"You have the same eyebrows."

"This is weird," she said. She may have had the same eyes and eyebrows as Jacob and the sheikh, but she was different from them. She was five feet three inches. The sheikh was about five feet ten inches and Jacob was about six feet tall. Her skin tone was different, too, more golden, less olive. Olivia shook her head. She did not want to think about the differences and similarities between herself and them.

Olivia looked at her watch. It was 7 p.m. "I'm tired. I think I will go lie down," she said. It had been such a long and eventful day. She needed to rest.

Chapter 3

Olivia woke with a fright. "What!" she breathed. Daya was standing over her.

"Sheikh Solomon is outside," she said.

Olivia sat up.

"He's what?"

"He came a few minutes ago and said that he wanted to speak with you."

Olivia looked at her wrist. It was six in the morning. "Why are you awake at this time?" she asked.

"I was on my way back from the bathroom when I saw him pacing around in the waiting area," said Daya. Olivia said nothing. She just climbed out of bed. She was still wearing her leggings and a T-shirt. Her hair was messy.

Olivia walked out of the room and into the sitting area. Sheikh Solomon was sitting on the sofa. "You wanted to see me," she said as she sat opposite him.

"I am sorry to interrupt your sleep," he replied.

"It's fine. The sooner we speak, the sooner I can return home." Olivia wondered how smoothly the talk was going to go. The first one had not gone so well.

"It was hard hearing about Elizabeth's passing."

"If you cared about her so much, then why did you not come after her?"

"It was complicated."

"So complicated that you let me grow up without a father? Maybe you are not my father."

"I did not know that she was pregnant."

Olivia raised her eyebrows. "You are lying," she said.

"I am not lying. She never told me. She just left."

"You slept with her? There is a chance that I am actually your daughter?"

Sheikh Solomon looked at Olivia's left wrist. "Jacob has the same birthmark on his left wrist," he said to her.

Olivia looked at her wrist. She had a small almond-shaped birthmark.

"That does not prove anything," she said.

"My mother has the same birthmark."

Olivia was silent for a moment. "I did not come here for recognition. I just wanted to understand how it was possible that my father was still alive and never came for me," she said.

"If I knew about you, I would have come for you," he said.

"I guess it does not matter anymore." She rose to her feet.

"It matters." Sheikh Solomon also rose to his feet. "I loved Elizabeth."

Olivia wanted to walk away. She just wanted to get her stuff and leave but she could not. She was filled with mixed emotions. Part of her did not want to believe that Sheikh Solomon did not know about her mother being pregnant, but she could see it in his eyes. He was not lying. His expression softened every time he said her mother's name. It made her wonder what had happened between them.

"How did you even meet her?" Olivia asked.

"She came here for a work placement," he replied. He folded his arms over his chest.

Olivia raised an eyebrow again.

"What kind of work?"

"She was on a scholarship. She was so intelligent and bright. Her university sent her over for a placement at my father's oil refinery." Sheikh Solomon smiled a little. Olivia could not believe her ears. Her mother had never told her about attending a university or going to the Middle East. It was all news to her.

"My mother studied engineering?" she asked.

"I guess there is a lot you do not know." Sheikh Solomon looked at his watch. "I have matters to attend to outside the city. Will you stay for a few days?"

"Here?" Olivia's eyes flew open.

"Yes. We have a lot to talk about."

"When will you return?"

"Tonight."

Olivia took a deep breath. "Fine, I'll stay. Just until tomorrow," she said. She really wanted to know about her mother's past. So she was willing to stay. Sheikh Solomon nodded. He turned on his heel and left.

***

A maid came to tell Daya and Olivia that breakfast was ready. She escorted them downstairs to the dining room. The dining room was big and elegantly decorated. There was large mahogany table in the middle of the room. A big chandelier hung from the ceiling above the table.

Olivia and Daya sat down at the table. The maids were still bringing the food out. Olivia felt weird about being in Sheikh Solomon's house while he was not there. She was grateful that Daya had come with her.

"Ah, you are still here," Jacob said as he walked into the room. He was wearing khaki chinos and a white polo shirt. He looked like a younger version of Sheikh Solomon. They both had olive skin tone.

"We are," Daya replied.

"Only until tomorrow," said Olivia.

Jacob sat down at the table.

"Tomorrow?" Jacob asked. He reached for a tangerine and started peeling it.

"After your father has returned from his trip."

Jacob studied Olivia as he peeled his tangerine. "Our father," he said. He started eating his tangerine.

"What?" Olivia asked.

"I guess you should say our father."

"I can't call him father. I did not come here for recognition."

Before Jacob could say anything else, two women walked in. They appeared to be in their early twenties. They were both slim. One was slightly taller than the other, about five foot seven. They both had long, straight jet-black hair. The taller one had her hair up in a ponytail and the other one had her hair down. They both had high cheekbones. They were beautiful but they looked unfriendly.

They both looked at Olivia and Daya. "Who are they?" the taller one asked Jacob. She pulled out a chair and sat down at the table. The other woman sat down next to her.

"This is about to get interesting," Jacob mumbled. He finished eating his tangerine and then wiped his hands on a napkin. "Olivia and…" He paused and looked at Daya.

"Daya," Daya said her name.

"This is Rania." He pointed at the taller woman. "And this is Marina. My younger sisters."

"Hello," Olivia greeted them.

"Are you my brother's guests?" Rania asked.

"She's our sister," Jacob said. He was not subtle. He went straight to the point and did not ease into the subject. He picked up the teapot and poured some tea into his cup.

"Excuse me?" said Marina.

"He's back at his tricks." Rania dismissed Jacob's words.

"I am not joking," said Jacob. Olivia did not feel like eating anymore. The air felt ominous. She did not see the breakfast ending well.

"What is he talking about?" Marina asked Olivia.

"Don't pay attention to his tricks," said Rania.

Olivia swallowed her food and spoke. "Apparently I am Sheikh Solomon's daughter. I found out a few days ago," she said. She was just like Jacob. She did not beat around the bush. She felt bad having to tell them. It would have been better if the sheikh had told them.

"This is ludicrous," said Rania.

"She probably wants money. People will say anything for money," Marina added.

"I do not want any money," said Olivia. She never wanted to be mistaken for an opportunist.

"Then what do you want?"

"Nothing. I do not want anything from your father."

Rania put her fork down. "I lost my appetite." She rose from the table. "You are not the first person to claim that you are our father's child. Just like the others, you will not succeed in your plans. Its best for you to give up now," she said.

"She doesn't even look anything like father. Pathetic," Marina added as she rose from the table. Marina and Rania both walked out of the room. Jacob smiled and shook his head. He took a sip of his tea.

"That was so uncomfortable," said Daya.

"There have been many people that came claiming to be our father's child. So you can understand why they won't even entertain this news," Jacob said.

"It doesn't matter. I will not be here long. I will be out of their lives by this time tomorrow," said Olivia.

"Hopefully you do not run into my mother or my sisters in the next twenty-four hours." Jacob rose from his chair. "If you will excuse me, I have a meeting to attend." Jacob headed out of the room.

"This trip is too much for me," Olivia said to Daya after Jacob had left the room. "I should not have come or I should have come at a different time."

"The outcome would have been the same, and if you did not come, you'd have spent your life wondering," said Daya.

"You are right but this family is too much for me. The mother and the girls are cold. I can't figure Jacob out."

"I can't figure him out either." Daya started eating some fruit. "I think he finds this situation amusing."

"He does." Olivia leaned back in her chair and took a deep breath. It was going to be a long day.

Chapter 4

Olivia had waited an entire day for the sheikh to return but he had returned well after she had fallen asleep. She figured that she would speak with him in the morning but then she heard that he was entertaining a guest. So she had no choice but to postpone her departure and wait until the sheikh was free.

In her loose-fitting, grey knee-length shorts and a white T-shirt, Olivia went for a walk in the garden. The sky was clear and the sun was nice and warm. It was a beautiful day. Olivia slid her hands in her pockets. She walked slowly, looking at the grass. She was so lost in her thoughts that she almost jumped out of her skin when Sheikh Solomon called out her name.

"Huh?" Olivia looked up. She saw Sheikh Solomon standing in the garden with an unfamiliar man. The man was wearing a crisp white shirt and a pair of grey trousers. He was tall. Taller than Sheikh Solomon, by at least five inches. His body was muscular. He had strong features. His almond-colored skin looked silky. He had jet-black hair cut short at the back and sides and just a hint of a beard. He had intense, dark green eyes. He was the most handsome man Olivia had ever laid eyes on. She wondered who he was.

"You are so deep in your thoughts," Sheikh Solomon said to her. "What is on your mind?"

"A lot of things," Olivia replied as she approached them.

"This is my daughter, Olivia," Sheikh Solomon said to the man he was standing with. "This is Sheikh Boutros," he said to her. The man raised his eyebrows slightly.

"Daughter," he repeated. His voice was so deep and smooth like silk. He looked at Olivia so intently.

"It's a long story," she said. It was clear that Sheikh Boutros was shocked upon hearing the news. Olivia did not want to go into detail about it, especially since she did not look at Sheikh Solomon as her father.

Just then, Daaliyah and her daughters walked outside. They were dressed elegantly in their expensive dresses and jewelry. They looked at Olivia with frowns on their faces. Daaliyah looked displeased to see her.

"Would you like to join us for tea?" Sheikh Solomon asked Olivia.

She shook her head.

"I won't impose. I will just return to my room." She smiled and left quickly.

***

Later that day, Sheikh Solomon asked his wife, Rania, Marina, Jacob, Olivia and even Daya to come meet with him in the living room. They all sat in the living room quietly for a moment. They were waiting for the sheikh to speak. The maid had served them with tea and cakes but no one was eating.

"Rania and Marina," said the sheikh.

"Yes, Father," they both replied.

"I understand you have already met Olivia. It would have been better if I had been the one to introduce you to her but it has already happened."

"Is she really your daughter?" Rania asked her father. Sheikh Solomon nodded.

"You are just going to accept her without a DNA test?" said Marina.

"What's the point? She looks like father," said Jacob.

"No, she does not," Rania protested.

"I am not going to accept her as my sister," said Marina.

"How old are you?" Rania asked Olivia.

"Twenty-three," Olivia replied. She did not like how Rania and Marina spoke about her and to her. However, she understood that they were angry.

"What?" Rania and Marina said at the same time.

"She is the same age as Jacob," Marina pointed out.

"You had two women pregnant at the same time?" Rania shouted at her father.

"Watch your tone," he warned. Daaliyah was not outraged about Olivia being the same age as Jacob. It made Olivia wonder why. A maid walked in with a landline telephone in her hand.

"Excuse me, sheikh," she said softly.

"Do you not see us in the middle of something?" Daaliyah snapped.

"I am sorry. The sheikh had previously instructed me to let him know when Sheikh Boutros called."

Daaliyah's eyes flew wide open. Rania and Marina both gasped and looked at the maid. Sheikh Solomon immediately took the phone from the maid. Olivia raised her eyebrows. She remembered Sheikh Boutros from earlier. She was curious as to why the mood changed when his name was mentioned.

"Hello, Sheikh Boutros," said Sheikh Solomon. His wife and his daughters had their eyes glued on him. "I did not expect to hear from you so soon," he continued. He went silent for a moment as he was listening to Sheikh Boutros.

"What?" said Sheikh Solomon. His eyes opened wide. "Really?" he asked. He went silent for a moment. "Are you sure?" he finally asked. He nodded. "I will let her know. Okay, goodbye."

"What did he say?" Daaliyah asked her husband.

"Who did he pick?" Marina asked. Sheikh Solomon remained silent. His face was strained with shock. He picked up his cup of tea and took a sip.

"Well, say something." Daaliyah was clearly getting impatient.

The sheikh took a deep breath.

"Olivia," he said quietly.

"Yes?" Olivia answered.

"Why are you bringing her into this when we are waiting for an answer?" Daaliyah asked.

"Sheikh Boutros picked Olivia," said Sheikh Solomon.

"What?" Daaliyah and her daughters shouted at once.

Jacob burst into laughter. "What an interesting turn of events," he said.

Olivia and Daya looked at each other. They were the only ones that did not know what was going on.

"Why on earth would he pick her?" Rania asked. Her face was turning red. She looked at Olivia. "Why did you have to come here?" she shouted at her.

Olivia looked at Sheikh Solomon for an answer.

"What is going on?" Daya asked.

"Basically Sheikh Boutros came here to pick a wife between my sisters and it seems that he wants to marry Olivia," Jacob explained. Marina frowned at him.

"What?" Olivia spat out.

"This man, Sheikh Boutros wants to marry Olivia? But he does not know her," said Daya.

"Exactly. How can he say that he wants to marry me? He only saw me for like two minutes."

"I will not allow this to happen. He has to marry one of my daughters," said Daaliyah. She looked at Olivia. "Shouldn't you be on your way back to America?" she asked her.

"As soon as I speak with Sheikh Solomon, I will head back," said Olivia.

"Can't you stay at a hotel or something?" Marina asked.

"That is enough," said Sheikh Solomon. "Olivia is my child and she is welcome in my home. As for Sheikh Boutros, he wishes to marry Olivia. I am just as shocked as all of you. However, it is his choice. So stop chastising Olivia about it."

"It does not matter what he wishes. I am not going to marry him. I will finish my business with Sheikh

Solomon and go back home. So you all can stop worrying about my presence," said Olivia. She rose to her feet and stalked to the exit.

Chapter 5

Sheikh Joseph Boutros slipped into his navy-blue shirt and black trousers. He headed downstairs, as he had been told by one of his maids that Sheikh Solomon had come to see him. Sheikh Boutros made his way into the drawing room where Sheikh Solomon waited for him. The drawing room was just a room used for entertaining guests. It was beautifully furnished with white sofas and purple pillows. There was a low wooden table that sat on a grey mat in the middle of the room. Expensive paintings hung on the white walls.

"Sheikh Boutros," said Sheikh Solomon as he rose from the sofa. He extended his hand for a handshake. Joseph shook his hand.

"Good to see you. Have a seat," said Joseph. The two men sat down on the sofas. "Would you like anything to drink or eat?"

"Oh no, please do not worry. I will not be staying for long."

"I suspect you came to see me about our last conversation." Joseph leaned back on his sofa.

Sheikh Solomon smiled and nodded.

"My daughter Olivia, she was not part of –" Sheikh Solomon stopped speaking. He was clearly speechless about Joseph's decision.

"I thought you only had two daughters. Olivia is from a different woman?"

"Yes. And I do not think your parents will be fine with you marrying an illegitimate daughter."

"You are right but it is my decision." Joseph was the type of man that did as he pleased. He never let others affect his decisions.

"If I may ask, why not Rania or Marina?" Sheikh Solomon asked.

"Upon seeing Olivia, I made my choice," he said. He had seen her walking in the garden. He watched her strolling while lost in her thoughts. She was beautiful. Her long brown waves had so much character. She had an oval-shaped face and gorgeous skin. Her body was nicely shaped like an hourglass. She was not dressed in a way that he would have approved on a woman but that could be changed.

"I see." Sheikh Solomon sighed. "I only just found out about her two days ago."

"Is that so?" Joseph raised his eyebrows. It was an intriguing situation.

"The last time I saw her mother was twenty-three years ago. I was surprised when Olivia came to my house and told me that she was my child."

"You believed her."

"I did."

"How is it that she only came to you now?"

"Her mother recently passed away. She apparently left her my details. The problem is that she wants to return to America. She does not want to have anything to do with me," said Sheikh Solomon. Joseph raised his eyebrows again. He thought it odd that after coming all this way, Olivia did not want to have anything to do with her father. Also, if she returned, then he would not be able to marry her. He definitely did not want either one of Sheikh Solomon's other daughters.

"That is not good news for me," said Joseph with a half-smile on his face.

Sheikh Solomon let out a laugh.

"She is an American girl. She is not likely to agree to this kind of marriage," he warned.

"I would like to invite her over for lunch," Joseph said. After spending time with him, Olivia would agree to stay and marry him. No woman had ever refused him.

"I will talk to her but I cannot promise anything." Sheikh Solomon sighed. There was no confidence in his words. He did not think he could convince Olivia to meet with Joseph for lunch.

The Boutros family and the Solomon family were close, especially Joseph's mother and Daaliyah. It had been discussed that Joseph would marry either Rania or Marina for some time. It would bring the two families closer and it would also benefit their businesses. The Boutros family owned the largest oil company in Lebanon. The Solomon family had a much smaller company but they produced a good quality of oil that sold at a high price. The Solomon family did not have enough capital to expand their business and joining their company with the Boutros company would allow them to expand. Both families would gain extra profits.

***

"We finally get to talk," Olivia said to her father. She had last spoken with him during what seemed to be a family meeting, even though she did not consider them to be her family. She had walked out after hearing that Sheikh Boutros wanted to marry her. So she had not gotten the chance to speak with Sheikh Solomon.

"Yes we do," said Sheikh Solomon. He picked up the jar of iced tea and poured some into their glasses. The two of them were having lunch in the garden.

"I will leave after we talk."

"You are so eager to leave. It hurts my feelings." Sheikh Solomon smiled.

"If I don't, my *sisters* will kill me." She said sisters sarcastically. Just like they did not see her as their sister, she did not see them as her sisters.

"This is your home too," said Sheikh Solomon.

Olivia raised her eyebrows as she picked up her fork. She started eating her lunch. She had to admit, the food tasted really good.

"I never knew that my mother studied engineering," Olivia said to the sheikh.

"Really?"

"She worked as a receptionist during the day and as a waitress at night. She worked two jobs just so that I could go to school. I wanted to work after high school. I wanted to share the burden but she would not let me," said Olivia. She felt sad thinking about how hard her mother had worked.

"You both lived a hard life." Sheikh Solomon sighed again.

"So how did you meet?"

"She was on a placement at my father's company just a few miles outside Beirut," he began to explain. "I had just started working there. My father had been grooming me to take over the company." Olivia listened as she ate.

"The first time I saw Ely, she was wearing rain boots that were too big for her." Sheikh Solomon started laughing. Olivia was shocked at hearing him refer to her mother as Ely. It seems he even had a pet name for her. "It had rained the night before. Therefore, the fields at the oil rig were muddy. Her boot got stuck in the mud."

"Then what happened?" Olivia asked. She was intrigued.

"She almost fell over but I caught her and helped her out of the mud." Sheikh Solomon took a sip of his tea. "She was always clumsy." He smiled.

Olivia laughed a little.

"Unfortunately for me, I inherited that trait from her," she said. The sheikh laughed. He spoke about her mother for a good twenty minutes. It was clear that he thought highly of her and never forgot about her. However, it still made no sense to Olivia how they had broken up. Why wasn't he aware of her pregnancy?

"I have to be at the office soon," the sheikh said to Olivia.

"You still haven't told me how she left or why she left without telling you that she was pregnant. What had happened? If the two of you were as close as you say you were, then she should have told you," Olivia replied.

"You will have to stay longer to find out."

Olivia narrowed her gaze at him. "You cannot use that to make me stay," she said to him. He smiled at her.

"It seems like this is the only thing I can do to spend some time with you. I have already missed out on twenty-three years," he said. Olivia shrugged her shoulders.

"There is something else I wish to discuss with you before I head to work," he added.

"What is it?" Olivia asked.

"Sheikh Boutros," Sheikh Solomon said quietly.

Olivia started laughing.

"We do not need to discuss him. There will be no marriage." She was not going to marry a man she barely knew. She thought it strange that he wanted to marry her.

"I went to see him this morning."

"You told him that I will not marry him?"

"He wants to meet with you for lunch."

Olivia looked at the sheikh with a blank expression. "Do I have to?" she asked.

"It may be better for you to refuse him yourself," said Sheikh Solomon.

"This is very strange to me. He saw me for a few seconds. We did not even speak beyond greetings, and now he wants to marry me."

"I understand. However, he is a good man and would make a great husband."

Olivia raised her eyebrows. "He may be a good man but we are two different people from different worlds. I am not willing to even consider the idea," she said. He was the most gorgeous man she had ever laid eyes on. However, it did not mean that she wanted to marry him.

"I understand your position. Perhaps you could just meet with him and tell him yourself," said Sheikh Solomon gently.

Olivia did not see why she had to. However, it seemed as though the Solomon family really valued and respected Sheikh Boutros. She had seen the way they all reacted when they heard that he was on the phone.

"I guess it would be polite for me to do so," said Olivia. "Besides, I am curious why he chose me."

Sheikh Solomon nodded. "I will have a driver take you tomorrow," he said with a smile. He looked as though he had won a battle. However, he had not.

Olivia was just going to go there and refuse his offer and then carry on with her life.

Chapter 6

"I don't even see why I should go," Olivia complained as she rummaged through her suitcase.

"Just think of it as a lunch date with an attractive man," said Daya. Olivia turned around and looked at Daya with a blank facial expression. "Well, you did say that he was good-looking, right?" Daya asked.

"He's okay."

"That isn't how you described him." Daya started laughing.

Olivia smiled and shook her head. She pulled out a short-sleeved, printed knee-length dress and quickly changed into it. She slipped into flat sandals. She untied her waves of hair and just finger combed it.

"Here I go," Olivia said.

"Okay, have fun," Daya replied.

Olivia headed out of her room and rushed downstairs. Just as Sheikh Solomon had said, there was a driver waiting for her. She got into the car. It was strange having a driver take her somewhere. She was used to taking the bus or riding her bike to places. This was new for her. She just sat in the backseat and looked out of the window.

As they drove into the city, Olivia's breath was taken away by its beauty. She wished she could explore Lebanon. She had never had the opportunity to travel to different countries. It was a shame that the first time she had left America, she was looking for a father she did not know existed.

Olivia arrived at the home of Sheikh Boutros almost twenty minutes later. They drove through large cast-iron gates. They drove up the driveway and parked outside a massive stone-colored mansion. It made Sheikh Solomon's house look pretty small.

"Is this a hotel?" Olivia asked.

"No, miss, this is Sheikh Boutros's residence," said the driver.

"Oh wow." Olivia was shocked. It was big enough to be a hotel. She just got out of the car and walked towards the house. She walked up the small flight of five stairs. A maid dressed in black and white opened the front door for Olivia.

"Miss Olivia Solomon?" the maid asked.

"No, Olivia Grant," she corrected her. She had not taken her father's name.

"My apologies. Come this way please." The maid turned and started walking. Olivia stepped into the house and followed the maid. She gasped when she saw the imperial-looking staircase in front of her. The stairs were white with brown wooden railings. A crystal chandelier hung from the high ceiling. The floor was made of white marble.

The maid headed down the wide hallway and then turned right. There large white double doors led into a big living room. The room had a beautiful cream and beige décor. There was a nice sitting area with cream tufted chairs with cream cushions. There were beautiful paintings hung on the wall. All the paintings had the same light brown frame that matched the furniture. There were glass double doors to the left leading to a courtyard.

"The sheikh will be with you in a moment," the maid said to Olivia.

"Okay," she replied. He should have been waiting for her, she thought to herself. She walked over to the glass doors and looked outside. There was a patio made of wood. There was a marble table with wooden chairs. The courtyard was large and filled with neatly cut green lawn and colorful flowers.

"You like the courtyard?" a deep voice sounded from behind Olivia. She turned around and found the tall, handsome sheikh standing before her. He was wearing a navy-blue shirt and charcoal grey trousers.

"It's not polite to make a lady wait," Olivia said to him.

The sheikh smiled at her.

"I'll keep that in mind for next time."

"There will be no next time. I am going back to Atlanta."

Sheikh Boutros raised his eyebrows. "Well, that's a shame," he said. He opened the glass doors and walked out onto the patio. "Lunch will be served in a moment." He gestured for Olivia to come out also. Olivia walked out onto the patio. The sheikh pulled out the chair her.

"Thank you," she said as she sat down. The sheikh sat opposite her. "What should I call you?" she asked.

"Sheikh Boutros," he replied.

Olivia narrowed her gaze at him.

"That is too long and too formal. What is your first name?"

"Joseph but only my family call me by my first name."

"Okay, I will call you Joseph for the next hour," she said. Joseph leaned back in his chair and just kept his eyes on Olivia. He looked amused. "What?" she asked. He just shook his head as if he had nothing to say but it was clear that he was thinking of something.

The maids walked out with trays of food. They carefully put the food on the table. They served traditional Arabic food and it looked quite appetizing. Olivia felt her mouth water. She was ready to start eating.

"So how come you are in such a rush to return to Atlanta?" Joseph asked Olivia. One of the maids poured them drinks before she left. Olivia reached out for her glass and took a sip. She did not know what kind of a drink it was, but it tasted good to her. So far, food and drinks were the only good things in Lebanon.

"Atlanta is my home and so I would like to return," Olivia replied vaguely. She picked up her fork and started eating.

"You came all this way to meet your father. You might as well stay and get to know him."

Olivia raised her eyebrows. She was surprised that Sheikh Solomon had told Joseph about her only finding out about him just recently. "Why do you want to marry me?" Olivia changed the subject.

"You are straightforward," said Joseph. He spoke so gently and his voice was so deep and alluring.

"I am."

"I like that."

Olivia was not sure how to respond to that. "My understanding is that you were to pick a wife between Rania and Marina," she said.

"I was to pick one of his daughters to be my betrothed."

"Betrothed." Olivia started laughing. "That is such an old word," Olivia added. Joseph did not respond immediately. He just ate and kept his gaze on her. "If I may ask, how old are you?" she asked.

"Are you curious?" he asked.

"I know nothing about you. That is the prime reason why I cannot marry you," she said. He barely removed his gaze from her. It made her slightly nervous because he had such intense, gorgeous green eyes.

"You can get to know me." He put a piece of meat in his mouth and chewed slowly.

Olivia found it a little seductive. She wanted to burst out laughing but she held back.

Instead, she said, "We are on different pages right now. I do not agree with arranged marriages. I am not even ready to be married right now."

"Are you in a relationship with anyone?"

"No, but that is beside the point." Olivia had actually never been in a proper relationship. Men had been interested in her but most only wanted to sleep with her. She had refused to sleep with anyone and therefore they had quickly lost interest in her. Others were not interested in her because she did not drink nor did she smoke. They found her to be plain.

"Perfect. I am not intruding," he replied. He picked up a napkin and wiped his mouth.

Olivia narrowed her gaze at him. Joseph was not exactly answering her questions. "So why an arranged marriage?" she asked.

"My mother and Daaliyah are close. So they wanted their children to wed," he replied.

"Well, I am not Daaliyah's daughter. So I do not count."

"You are Sheikh Solomon's daughter and the arrangement was to marry one of his daughters."

Olivia sighed and ran her hand through her hair. She leaned back in her chair. "Why me then?" she asked.

"You are the most beautiful one out of the three and there is something intriguing about you," he said so seductively.

Olivia pressed her knees together. She was thinking maybe it was her lack of experience with men that made her find everything about him so seductive. "There is nothing intriguing about me. I am just your ordinary plain Jane," she said. She took a sip of her drink. "Thank you for the lunch, Joseph. I guess we will not be seeing each other after this."

Joseph picked up his glass and slowly drank from it. He put the glass down.

"There is nothing plain about you," he said.

Olivia was surprised that he did not think she was plain. She felt her stomach knotting up. It was crazy to her how he stirred so many emotions within her.

"There is. You just do not know much about me," she said. She wasn't sure what to say. It was unlike her to be speechless and yet in front of Joseph, it kept happening.

"I don't. So you have to give me the chance to get to know you," he replied.

Olivia was feeling very awkward. In a different circumstance, she would have wanted to go on dates with him. However, it was not like that right now. This meant staying in Sheikh Solomon's house longer and she did not want that.

Olivia rose to her feet. Joseph stood up seconds after her. "Well, that is going to be hard when I am on the other side of the world," Olivia said to him. Joseph grunted. He gestured towards the glass doors. He and Olivia walked through them.

"When are you leaving?" Joseph asked her.

"Hopefully tomorrow. I still need to speak to Sheikh Solomon. There is a side of my mother that he knew that I did not know. I'm also curious about how they split. Why did she not tell him about me?" Olivia replied.

"I understand but isn't tomorrow too soon? You need to spend a few days with him at least," said Joseph as they headed into the hallway.

"This is all too much for me at the moment. My mother passed away not too long ago and then I found out that I have a father. I don't know how to deal with it. Going back home will be good for me. That's my comfort zone," said Olivia.

"Going back now will deny you the opportunity to get to know him."

Olivia sighed. "I know you are right but it's uncomfortable living in the same house as my new half-sisters that do not like me."

"They probably feel as confused as you are," Joseph replied. They stopped at the front door.

Olivia looked at him with a blank facial expression.

"I am in a worse position. They could be more sympathetic," she said.

"Dinner tomorrow?"

"What?"

"Let's have dinner tomorrow," he said confidently.

"I will not be here tomorrow night," Olivia replied matter-of-factly.

"You have a lot you wish to get off your chest. We can talk more tomorrow over dinner while I get to know you." Joseph smiled. His smile almost melted her insides. Olivia just walked out quickly.

Chapter 7

Joseph was in his home office looking over some paperwork later that day. Thoughts of Olivia kept entering his mind. She was just so intriguing to him. She had tried to ward him off but he was not going to allow her to do so. Whenever he wanted something, he would do whatever it took to get it. He did not take no for answer.

"Joseph!" a voice sounded from the hallway. Joseph immediately knew whose voice it was. He leaned back in his white leather chair and looked at the door. His mother walked in moments later.

"Hello, Mother," he replied.

She smiled and approached him. She kissed him on both cheeks.

"How are you?" she asked as she sat down opposite him. She sat up straight and clasped her hands together. She was so poised and so regal. She wore a white dress and elegant pearls. She had olive skin color.

"I am well," Joseph replied.

"I am curious."

"About what?" Joseph knew exactly what his mother was curious about.

"Rania or Marina?" his mother asked.

Joseph grunted.

"We will be meeting with their family soon. You might have to wait until then." Joseph was not sure it was his place to tell his mother about Olivia. He wanted her to hear from Sheikh Solomon that he had an illegitimate daughter.

"You have not made a decision?" she asked.

"Something like that."

"That is unlike you." His mother looked surprised. "What is wrong with the girls?" she asked.

"Nothing. I guess I have not spent much time with them to get to know them." Joseph immediately frowned. It was as if he was regurgitating Olivia's words.

His mother also looked shocked to hear his words.

"What else do you need to know? They're both from a good family. They are beautiful and well-educated," she said to him.

Joseph did not agree. To him, they were average-looking.

"Shall we have dinner?" he asked.

"Why are you changing the subject?"

"I am just hungry." Joseph smiled. His mother was invested in that marriage. She really wanted him to marry either Rania or Marina. Therefore, she was going to keep talking about it. So Joseph thought it best to change the subject. He wanted to wait until she found out about Olivia's existence before he told her that he wanted to marry Olivia.

***

"Sheikh Boutros, thank you for coming." Sheikh Solomon greeted him with a smile. He shook Joseph's hand. Joseph had decided to go to Sheikh Solomon's house the following evening. He needed to talk to him. Olivia had stood him up. She had not gone to his house for dinner. No woman had ever turned him down for anything.

"I trust that you have been well," Joseph said to Sheikh Solomon.

"I have. Please have a seat."

The two men sat down in the drawing room. A maid served them with tea and cakes. Joseph picked up his cup of tea and took a sip.

"My mother dropped by my house last night," Joseph said to Sheikh Solomon. "I have not told her about Olivia's existence yet. I feel that it should come from yourself."

"It is going to be tough talking about it. Having an illegitimate child is never a good look, especially for a sheikh," said Sheikh Solomon.

"Yes, it will be tough. It must already be tough on your family."

"My wife and my daughters are not taking it well."

"I take it they're not welcoming Olivia?" Joseph asked. He already knew that they were not. He had heard from Olivia.

Sheikh Solomon laughed.

"It has only been three days but it feels ominous in this house. We are walking on eggshells." Sheikh Solomon laughed again. This time Joseph laughed with him.

"They're all going through a hard time. This is something that came upon all of you so suddenly," Joseph said.

"Exactly."

"Sheikh Boutros," Rania breathed out as she walked into the room. She was wearing a peach dress and a pair of white high heels.

"Hello Rania," he replied. She stood by her father, facing Joseph. She had her chest perked up and her lips pouted.

"It's good to see you," she said.

"Likewise."

"I will let the two of you speak. Sheikh Boutros, please come over for dinner sometime." She ran her hand through her jet-black hair and smiled at him. She turned on her heel and walked out. Joseph wondered if she knew that he wanted to marry Olivia instead of her or her sister. She was quite flirtatious and obviously wanted his attention.

"Is Olivia still here?" Joseph asked.

"Yes, she is still here. She says we have a lot to talk about, which we do. So I am glad that she is going to stay," Sheikh Solomon replied just as Marina rushed into the room. She was wearing a tight-fitting yellow dress. She had long, silky jet-back hair.

"Sheikh Boutros, it's good to see you," she said as she approached him. She extended her hand out for a handshake.

"Hello Marina." Joseph shook her hand. Marina giggled when he touched her hand. Sheikh Solomon buried his face in his hands.

"If only you had come earlier for dinner," she said to him.

"Maybe next time."

"Yes. That will be nice. Come for lunch and dinner."

"Okay Marina, if you could give us a moment," Sheikh Solomon said to his overly excited daughter.

"Okay. It was good to see you, Sheikh Boutros. Take care." She turned and left the room.

"Do they know that I have already made my decision regarding marriage?" Joseph asked Sheikh Solomon after Marina had left.

"They do but they just do not accept it." Sheikh Solomon shook his head. Joseph was not surprised. He was used to women doing everything they could to be with him.

The two men started discussing business. As they were talking, Olivia walked past the drawing room. Once again, she was wearing loose-fitting shorts and a loose-fitting top. Her hair was messy.

"Olivia!" Sheikh Solomon called out. She walked back and into the room. "Come and greet Sheikh Boutros," he said to her. Olivia was looking at him as if she was going to ask if she had to.

"Good evening, Miss Grant," Joseph said to Olivia.

"Sheikh Boutros," said Olivia. It was interesting to Joseph that Rania and Marina were impeccably dressed, and Olivia was not. However, Olivia looked better than the other two. He wondered how she would look if she properly dressed herself.

One of the maids rushed into the room.

"Excuse me, Sheikh Solomon. You have an urgent call," the maid said to Sheikh Solomon. He nodded and rose to his feet.

"If you would excuse me for a moment," he said to Joseph and left the room. Joseph leaned in his seat and fixed his gaze on Olivia.

"I guess it's just the two of us," he said to her.

Chapter 8

"Goodbye, Joseph," Olivia said to Sheikh Boutros. She was surprised to see him at Sheikh Solomon's house. He had asked to have dinner with her that night but she had stood him up. It was awkward seeing him now.

"You stood me up," he said to her.

Olivia slid her hands in her pockets and looked at him. "I told you that I was not coming."

"No one has ever stood me up."

"There is a first time for everything." It was hard to keep eye contact with Joseph. His intense gaze made Olivia nervous.

"I see you decided to take my advice," said Joseph. He had a smug look on his face. It was as if he had won something.

"What advice?" Olivia asked.

"To stay here."

"Oh. That had nothing to do with you," she replied. Joseph said nothing for a moment. He looked amused. "What?" she asked. It was not the first time he had looked at her like that.

"How long will you stay?" he asked.

"Just a few days." It was annoying that she had had to reschedule her departure so many times. However, Daya, Sheikh Solomon and Joseph all gave her good reasons to stay. It was a very hard situation for her to deal with. She did not know what to do. She wished her mother was still alive. She wished that she could talk to her.

"That gives us enough time to get to know each other," said Joseph.

Olivia narrowed her gaze at him. He was relentless.

"Spending time together will not change anything. We are not getting married." Olivia turned away from him and headed for the door. If he had been asking her only for a date, then she would have agreed. However, he was asking for her hand in marriage. Why did the good-looking guys have to be so weird?

"How impertinent of you to walk away in the middle of the conversation," Joseph said to Olivia.

"Excuse me?" She turned around to face him. Did he just call me impertinent? Olivia asked herself.

"We were still in the middle of a conversation. It is rude for you to just walk away," said Joseph. Olivia raised her eyebrows. She had not realized that there was still more to talk about. "And shouldn't you dress a little bit more feminine?" he added.

Olivia looked at her attire.

"There is nothing wrong with my clothes," she said to him. Joseph made a face. "I don't care what you think of my dress sense. You trying to tell me how to dress just made me not want to marry you even more." Olivia turned away from him and left the drawing room.

Olivia was annoyed at Joseph for making a comment about her clothes. He had no right to do so. She was never going to marry a man that tried to control her in any way. She rushed up the stairs and saw Daya sitting outside their bedrooms.

"Guess who is here?" Olivia asked Daya.

"Joseph Boutros?" Daya looked up from her magazine.

"He had the nerve to tell me to dress a little bit more feminine." Olivia threw herself on the sofa opposite Daya.

"What?" Daya laughed a little. "He did?" she asked.

"He is relentless. I told him countless times that I did not want to marry him but he just refuses to hear me."

"You are crazy."

"What?"

"If he is as handsome as you say he is, then why don't you spend some time with him? Just enjoy being in his company," said Daya.

Olivia rolled her eyes.

"He is handsome and a little arrogant. I do not want to spend time with a man like that," said Olivia.

"Was he here to see you?" Daya asked.

"No, he came for Sheikh Solomon."

***

The next morning was easily the worst morning Olivia had in Sheikh Solomon's house. He had called everyone downstairs for breakfast. He wanted his entire family to have breakfast together. He wanted them all to get along but Olivia felt that it was too soon. Things never worked out well when forced.

"Must we eat with her?" Rania asked her father.

"From now on, we will eat together," said Sheikh Solomon. All the women at the table looked at him as though he was crazy.

"That isn't the wisest of your decisions," Jacob said to his father.

"We are a family whether anyone likes it or not." Sheikh Solomon took a deep breath. "We have been invited to the Boutros residence on Sunday," he added.

"Who is we?" Daaliyah asked her husband.

"Everyone sitting at this table."

"Why is that one coming?" Rania pointed at Daya. "She is not even part of the family."

"That one?" said Olivia. Her so-called sisters were so rude.

"Yes, that!"

"You are so rude." Even though Olivia knew that she was guest in their home, she was not going to be silent while Rania and Marina were rude to Daya. It was uncalled for and unnecessary.

"And you are an intruder," said Marina.

"You are not welcome here," Rania said to Olivia.

"I can stay here. I do not have to come on Sunday," said Daya. "However, Olivia is not an intruder and you have no right to be so rude to her," she added. Daya and Olivia were so close. They were always on each other's side.

Rania and Marina both started speaking at the same time. They voiced their displeasure. Daya and Olivia had no choice but to answer. They too voiced their displeasure. It was like a screaming match. Jacob just leaned back in his chair and watched.

Sheikh Solomon dropped his fork.

"Enough!" he shouted. "I will not have the four of you fighting, especially at the breakfast table."

Olivia could not believe that she was taking part in the fighting. It was unlike her. She did not like drama and arguments. However, Rania and Marina seemed to bring out the worst in her.

"There would not be any fighting if you did not have an illegitimate child," said Daaliyah. Sheikh Solomon shot her a warning gaze.

"We are happy to stay in a hotel and to not come on Sunday," said Olivia.

"You are not staying in a hotel and you are most certainly coming on Sunday."

Olivia did not like taking orders from anyone. She did not want to go to the Boutros residence. She did not see the point of her going. However, she was not going to take it up with Sheikh Solomon at that moment. She just narrowed her gaze at him and bit her tongue.

"It will be a very interesting day," Jacob added. He took a sip of his coffee.

"We should all eat in silence," said Sheikh Solomon. Olivia thought he was probably regretting the idea of getting everyone to dine together. It was definitely too soon for them to act as though they were family.

Chapter 9

There was a knock on Joseph's office door. "Come in," Joseph called out. The door opened and his cousin Amir walked in. The two of them had been so close growing up. Joseph welcomed him with a warm smile.

"Joseph Boutros," Amir said as he walked into the clinically clean office. Joseph was very smart and particular about his work, so everything had to be clean and tidy. His office had a beautiful grey décor. It had big windows.

"How was your trip?" Joseph asked Amir.

"It was productive." Amir sat in the grey tufted chair at Joseph's desk. "So, you met with the Solomon girls?"

Joseph narrowed his gaze at Amir. "That had to be the first thing you had to mention," he said to him.

"Of course. You need to be married soon."

Joseph ran his hand through his hair and leaned back into his chair. Amir was right. He needed to be married before he turned thirty years old. That was the condition that his father had stipulated. Joseph was to be married by age thirty if he wanted to inherit his father's oil business. His father wanted him to settle down and have a family. Joseph wasn't the settling down type. He enjoyed his bachelor lifestyle too much. To make matters worse, his mother wanted him to marry one of Sheikh Solomon's daughters.

"I have about three months to get married," said Joseph.

"That is plenty of time. Your mother has already provided you with choices. You just have to pick one and then that's it," said Amir.

"I went to Sheikh Solomon's house and found out that he had another daughter."

"Other than Rania and Marina?"

"Yes. He has an illegitimate child."

Amir's eyes opened wide. "How did he manage to keep her hidden for so long?"

"He only just found out about her."

"Well, that makes sense. So who did you pick between Rania and Marina?"

"Neither one of them."

Amir raised an eyebrow. "You did not?" He looked so confused.

"I told Sheikh Solomon that I wanted to marry his illegitimate daughter Olivia," said Joseph.

Amir leaned forward.

"What?" he asked. He ran his hand through his wavy brown hair.

"She is much better-looking than the other two."

"Is that wise? You know how traditional your parents are," Amir pointed out. He was quite right. Joseph's parents were traditional. They were not going to like Joseph's decision to marry Olivia.

"My mother said to marry one of Sheikh Solomon's daughters. Olivia is one of Sheikh Solomon's daughters."

Amir started laughing. "You want to use her words against her," he said. Joseph smiled. "But do tell, how much better-looking is Olivia than the other two?" Amir asked.

"She has a much curvier figure."

"That sounds indulging," Amir said mischievously.

Joseph chuckled a little.

"I admit her body is quite tempting. She is also beautiful but the problem is her dressing." Joseph could not lie that the thought of her naked body on his bed had not crossed his mind. She had an amazing body.

"Is she Arabic?" Amir asked.

"Half-Arabic."

"That is even worse! Your mother will not stand for that."

"I know. Anyway the marriage will not last long." Joseph was not all that bothered. He just wanted to get married and inherit his father's company. His plan was to get married and then get divorced after three years.

"What if you fell in love with her?" Amir asked. Joseph raised his eyebrows before bursting into laughter. Amir laughed also. "Of course, this is you we are talking about," he added. Joseph thought love was frivolous. He did not want to waste his time on such things. In the past, all the women that had claimed to love him only wanted his money.

"Exactly, that will not happen," said Joseph.

"What if you have a baby?"

"That is even better. If we have a child, then my parents will know that I tried. I will also have an heir."

Amir shook his head.

"The Solomons are going over to my parents' house on Sunday," said Joseph.

"This Sunday?" Amir asked.

"Yes and you should come."

"Of course I will come. I want to see your new bride. She will be there, right?"

Joseph nodded. "Sheikh Solomon told me that he will bring her so that he can introduce her to my parents."

"There will be fireworks," said Amir. It was not a secret how strict Joseph's parents were. They had an impeccable reputation. They were definitely not going to agree with the idea of their only son marrying an illegitimate child that wasn't even full Arabic.

"We have a meeting soon. We should eat before then," Joseph suggested as he rose to his feet. Amir also worked at the Boutros oil company. Both Amir and Joseph had studied oil and gas engineering. They oversaw all the projects at the company. It was their duty to make sure that everything went smoothly from the drilling to the exporting.

"I am actually quite famished," said Amir as he rose to his feet also. The two of them headed out of Joseph's office. Amir was about two inches shorter than Joseph. They had similar muscular physiques. Amir's hair was a few inches longer than Joseph's. Also Joseph had jet-black hair and Amir had dark brown hair. Their mothers were sisters but they looked like each other a lot. People often thought they were brothers.

"Hold my calls. I will be going out for lunch," Joseph said to his assistant Tamar.

"Yes sir," she replied. She tucked a lock of hair behind her ear. "Is there anything else I can do for you?" she asked. She looked too eager to do something for him.

"No." Joseph slid in his hands in his pockets and walked off. Amir walked off with him.

"Are you sleeping with her?" Amir asked Joseph.

"Am I sleeping with who?" Joseph asked.

"Your assistant."

"Tamar? No, I am not sleeping with her."

"Then why does she look at you with hearts in her eyes?"

Joseph chuckled a little. "Every woman that isn't related to me looks at me with hearts in her eyes," he said.

"Does Olivia?" Amir asked.

"She is a different type of woman. She actually had the nerve to stand me up." Joseph was not pleased about that. He was both intrigued and annoyed by it.

Amir whipped his head in Joseph's direction.

"She stood you up? Really?" Amir was clearly shocked. "No woman has ever done that."

"Exactly."

"I am even more interested in meeting her."

Two women walked past Amir and Joseph. They had their eyes glued on Joseph with big smiles across their faces. Joseph barely looked at them. He just walked past them. Having women stare at him was nothing new. He was used to it.

Chapter 10

It was Friday and Olivia was bored. She did not want to spend the day inside the house, especially since Rania and Marina were at home. It was just so uncomfortable being around them. They always ended up being in some kind of argument. So Olivia suggested that she and Daya go to explore Beirut, the capital city of Lebanon.

Olivia and Daya walked out of Sheikh Solomon's mansion and out into the warm Middle Eastern sun. Jacob was leaning against his black Bentley. He had his phone in his hand. He looked up from his phone and saw Olivia and Daya walking out of the house.

"Where are you two off to?" he asked.

"Sightseeing," Olivia replied. She was not quite sure about how she felt about Jacob. He hadn't been as nasty as his sisters had been to Olivia.

"I thought you were going shopping."

"Why shopping?"

"You will be seeing your husband-to-be in two days."

Olivia narrowed her gaze at Jacob. "He is not going to be my husband," she replied.

Jacob slid his phone in his pocket.

"Why not? There are tons of women dying to be his wife, my sisters included," he said.

Olivia rolled her big hazel eyes.

"Then he can choose a wife from all those women. I myself am not interested in marrying a man I know nothing about," said Olivia.

"He is a good man," said Jacob.

"So you also think I should marry him." Olivia narrowed her gaze at Jacob.

"No, I am just pointing out good things about him."

"Shouldn't you be trying get him hitched to one your sisters?" Olivia asked. If Joseph was a good man as Jacob said he was, then surely he would want one of his sisters to marry him.

Jacob shrugged his shoulders. "Of course it would be good if he married Rania or Marina but frankly I do not care about all of that," said Jacob. He pulled out his phone and looked at it.

"You seem rather amused by all of this actually," Daya pointed out.

Jacob smiled.

"I am," he admitted.

"Are you going into the city?" Olivia asked.

"Um –"

Before Jacob could say anything else, Olivia cut him off. "Ah, that's good. Perhaps you could give us a lift," she said with a big grin plastered across her face.

Jacob raised his dark eyebrows.

"Why would I do that?" he asked.

"Because you are the kindest of the Solomons."

"I will have my driver take you where you need to go. I have matters to attend to," said Jacob.

"Matters that concern the person you are messaging," Olivia said cheekily. He slid his phone back into his pocket and looked at Olivia. He said nothing as he walked off.

The driver appeared moments later. He unlocked the door for Olivia and Daya. The two of them climbed into the backseat. Olivia sat comfortably in the beige leather seat. It was so comfortable and spacious inside the car. Inside Jacob's car. She had asked him to drive her and Daya into the city to see how he would react. She was unsure of his position in regards to her.

They reached the city no more than ten minutes later. Sheikh Solomon lived just on the outskirts of Beirut. The driver dropped off Olivia and Daya outside a large shopping mall. The mall was massive and clean. There were small palm trees in the mall.

Olivia had never seen trees in a mall but it was nice. The mall was different from malls in Atlanta.

"We should go eat first," Olivia said to Daya.

Her friend laughed.

"Of course you would say that," Daya replied. Olivia always wanted to eat. "I am just going to use the restroom first." Daya scurried off to the restrooms. Olivia slipped her hands in her jeans and walked towards the railings. She stood there looking around.

"Miss Grant," a voice sounded from behind Olivia. It startled her a little bit. She turned around sharply and found Joseph standing before her. He was wearing a tab-collared navy-blue shirt and black tailored trousers. He looked good as always.

"Joseph," Olivia breathed.

Joseph narrowed his gaze at her.

"You're still not referring to me as Sheikh Boutros."

Olivia smiled and shrugged her shoulders. "It's such a long title," she said. He did not look all that pleased.

"It's just two words. Try saying it just once," he said.

"Sheikh Boutros." She decided to humor him. He smiled.

"We will work on your pronunciation later." Joseph spoke seductively or maybe it was just how Olivia was hearing his voice.

"This is why I should keep calling you Joseph."

"You're here for shopping?"

"Just sightseeing."

"I thought you were buying an outfit for when you meet my family on Sunday," said Joseph.

Olivia raised her eyebrows.

"Who said that I am coming?" she asked. She did not want to go because she did not see the point of her presence.

"Your father."

"I do not understand why I should I attend."

Joseph raised his eyebrows slowly. "You will be meeting your future in-laws," he said.

Olivia burst out laughing.

"My future in-laws," she repeated. She shook her head. "I feel as though I stepped into the Twilight Zone or something," she added.

"What?"

"This is an odd reality. These kinds of marriages are normal to you all but not to me. I am tired of having the same conversation again and again. There will be no marriage. I will not marry you," she said.

Joseph slipped his hands in his pockets.

"Dinner tomorrow night," said Joseph.

Olivia crossed her eyebrows.

"What?"

"We should have dinner tomorrow."

"I thought you would have learned from last time."

"It's just food," Joseph said as if she was reading too much into the situation.

"It's food with you," said Olivia.

"And what is wrong with that?"

Olivia sighed. "I will see you on Sunday, Joseph," she said to him.

He smiled and took a step closer to her. He dipped his head and moved it closer to Olivia's face. "What are you doing?" Olivia took a step back.

"I don't make the habit to ask twice," he said. His voice was suddenly deeper. It made Olivia a little nervous but intrigued.

"And yet you did," she replied softly.

Joseph slowly scanned her face before he said anything.

"See you on Sunday," he said. "Wear a dress." Joseph turned and walked off. Olivia exhaled loudly. Joseph made her nervous. She hoped that he did not notice. He seemed like he was the type of man to gloat about having an effect on a woman.

Daya suddenly appeared. Olivia had been so consumed in her thoughts about Joseph that she had not seen Daya approaching. "Let's go find food," Daya said to Olivia.

"You scared me," said Olivia.

"Why are you so deep in thought? What's on your mind?"

"Joseph was just here," Olivia said as they started walking.

"Joseph? As in Sheikh Boutros?" Daya asked.

"Yes."

"Why do I keep missing him?"

"Why are you eager to see him?"

"I want to know what he looks like. I want to see why everyone is so obsessed with this man," said Daya.

"Everyone but me," Olivia clarified.

"What did you talk about?

Daya and Olivia walked into the food court. "As usual he cut me off when I was saying that I am not going to marry him and started talking about something else," said Olivia.

"What did he change the subject to?"

"Dinner. He wanted to have dinner tomorrow night."

"And you said no," said Daya. They both stopped at a restaurant.

"Of course I did." Olivia crossed her arms over her chest.

"This entire situation is a bit comedic," said Daya. "He met you once and now he is so intent on marrying you. I really need to see this man."

"I guess you will see him on Sunday," said Olivia. It seemed that there was no way for her to avoid going to meet Joseph's family. If she was going to go, she was going to need Daya by her side.

"You've decided to go?" Daya asked.

Olivia shrugged her shoulders.

"I don't want to go but Sheikh Solomon really wants me to go. I guess I can understand why," she replied. Her father wanted to tell the Boutros family about her. She was surprised that he was quick to accept her as his daughter. Olivia knew that she did not owe Sheikh Solomon anything. Most of her wanted to just go back to Atlanta and forget his existence. However, part of her wanted to know what he was like, what her mother had seen in him and why they had broken up.

Chapter 11

"Good afternoon," a tall beautiful woman said as she walked into the Boutros's large cream and beige drawing room. She was wearing a peach boatneck dress and low heels. She had her silky jet-black hair tied up into a neat bun.

"Jasmine," Joseph said with a smile. He rose to his feet. He walked across the wooden floor and approached her. He held her shoulders and kissed her cheeks. "This is a pleasant surprise," he added.

"Surprise? Today is the day that we meet your wife-to-be. Of course I came," she said and wiggled her eyebrows. Jasmine was Amir's twin sister.

Joseph looked at Amir.

"You told her," Joseph said to Amir.

"Told her what?" Joseph's mother Esther said as she walked into the room. She wore an ankle-length, long-sleeved sky-blue dress. She wore a pearl necklace and matching pearl earrings. She looked as elegant as always.

"Aunty Esther," Jasmine said with a big smile on her face. The two women hugged and kissed each other on both cheeks.

"I'm glad you came," said Esther.

"Of course, it's an important day." Jasmine looked at Joseph and grinned.

"Is there something I should know?" Esther looked at her son.

"No." Joseph shook his head. It was clear that Amir had told Jasmine about Olivia. There were no secrets between the three of them. Joseph definitely did not want to divulge the information to his mother, not until Sheikh Solomon had told her about Olivia.

"Of course I told her." Amir rose from his seat and approached his sister. He kissed her on both cheeks. "How was Egypt?" he asked her. Jasmine had been in Egypt doing some charity work. She enjoyed working with different charities building schools and hospitals, teaching English, teaching how to read and write.

"It was great," she replied. "But I think this dinner will be better."

"Don't cause trouble," Joseph warned. Jasmine was mischievous and liked stirring the pot a little. Jasmine laughed and crossed her arms over her chest.

A maid walked into the room.

"May I present the Solomons," she said. Jasmine and Amir looked at Joseph and smiled.

"Here we go," said Jasmine.

Sheikh Solomon and his wife walked into the room. Esther immediately went to greet Sheikh Solomon's wife.

"Daaliyah," Esther said joyfully.

"Esther, it's good to see you," she replied. The two women embraced each other and kissed each other on both cheeks.

"Sheikh Solomon, I trust that you have been well," Esther greeted Sheikh Solomon. He smiled and kissed her on both cheeks.

"I have, thank you. It's good to see you," he replied.

"My husband is just upstairs changing. He came back late from his business trip. He won't be a moment."

"I understand."

Joseph saw Sheikh Solomon's children and an unfamiliar woman walking into the room. To his surprise, Olivia was wearing a dress. She wore a knee-length, short-sleeved black dress. It hugged her curves seductively. The dress revealed her hourglass figure and her beautiful legs. She wore platform wedges with the dress. She had no makeup and no jewelry on. Her long waves of brown tresses framed her face.

"Is that her?" Jasmine and Amir whispered to Joseph at the same time. Joseph did not bother responding. He just shook his head. Jacob approached Joseph and greeted him. He also greeted Amir and Jasmine.

"You girls have grown," Esther said to Rania and Marina. She turned her attention to Jacob. "And you my dear, you have grown handsome," she said to him.

"Thank you," Jacob replied with a smile.

Daaliyah approached Joseph with a smile. She greeted him and then greeted Amir and Jasmine.

"Your… guests?" Esther asked Sheikh Solomon. He took a deep breath before he replied.

"Yes," he said.

"Oh." Esther looked confused. She probably wanted to ask why they had come to her house. She looked at Olivia and Daya. "Hello," she said to them.

"Hello, Mrs. Boutros," Olivia and Daya said at the same time. They both smiled at her.

Joseph's father walked into the room.

"I apologize for being tardy," Sheikh Boutros senior said. Joseph looked like his father. They were both tall and handsome. His father had some grey in his hair. His presence was very noticeable, very demanding.

"It's no problem, sheikh," said Daaliyah.

"I trust that you have been well," he said to Sheikh Solomon and shook his hand.

"I've been well, thank you," Sheikh Solomon replied. He looked at Sheikh Boutros senior with so much respect in his eyes.

Olivia looked up and found Joseph staring at her. She looked away and looked back, he was still looking at her. He slipped his hands in his pockets and allowed his gaze to wash over her slowly. She crossed her eyebrows. She looked as though she was going to ask him why he was looking at her.

A maid walked in and announced that lunch was ready. They all made their way to the dining room. Joseph's father looked at Olivia and Daya as they walked into the dining room. He raised his eyebrows. "I don't think we've met," he said.

"I am Olivia." She extended her hand for a handshake.

Joseph's father shook her hand with a smile.

"Hello Olivia." He turned his attention to Daya. "And who is this young lady?"

"My name is Daya." She smiled and shook his hand. Rania and Marina were watching Olivia and Daya. They did not look happy.

***

Joseph's father sat at the head of the table. His wife sat to his right. Sheikh Solomon sat to his left. His wife sat next to him. Joseph sat opposite from his father. Amir sat to his left and Jasmine to his right. Olivia sat next to Jasmine. Joseph could see Olivia perfectly.

They all sat at the large, intricately designed, marble-topped dining table. A large crystal chandelier hung above the table. There was a variety of delicious and appetizing food on the table.

Naturally, the two older men started talking about business. They were both passionate about the oil business and were always looking for a way to expand their companies. Joseph, Amir and Jacob contributed to the conversation. They women just quietly agreed and kept eating. Joseph spotted Olivia and the unfamiliar woman she had come with whispering to each other.

Joseph wondered if she was Olivia's cousin as they seemed so close. Jasmine leaned closer to Olivia and said something to her. Joseph wondered what she had said to her. Olivia faced Jasmine and smiled before she responded. She briefly made eye contact with Joseph, and then looked away.

The lunch was going well until Esther brought up the marriage issue. "Rania and Marina have grown into beautiful young ladies," she said. "Don't you think so, Joseph?"

Joseph smiled and took a sip of his drink. He did not want to answer her question because to him, Rania and Marina were just average. Amir looked at him and smiled. "It's unfortunate that he has to make a choice between them," he said. Joseph narrowed his gaze at him.

"You are right," Esther said and laughed a little.

"Perhaps it would have been easier if he was to marry the eldest daughter," said Jasmine. Joseph crossed his eyebrows subtly enough to warn Jasmine but not enough for Rania and Marina to notice. They were both staring at Joseph; smiling and tucking their hair behind their ears.

"There is something I must tell you all," Sheikh Solomon said. He cleared his throat and squared his shoulders. Everyone whipped their heads in his direction. His wife looked uncomfortable.

"What is it?" Joseph's father asked him. Sheikh Solomon cleared his throat again. Marina and Rania looked at each other. The atmosphere was thick with awkwardness.

"Olivia is my daughter." He went straight to the point.

Esther gasped and placed her hand on her chest.

"Excuse me?" she spat out.

Joseph's father leaned forward in his seat.

"She is your daughter?" He looked at Olivia. She was just sitting there drinking her juice and trying not to get involved, as if that was possible. She was the center of the conversation.

"Yes, she is," said Sheikh Solomon.

Esther pressed her palm against her forehead and leaned back into her chair. "That is not possible," Esther said. It was clear that she was still trying to stay elegant but she was in shock. She did not seem pleased either. Joseph looked at Olivia. She seemed calm.

"Perhaps this is a conversation we should have in private," said Joseph's father. Rania looked at Olivia with a frown on her face. She looked as though she was angry at Olivia for existing.

"You were unfaithful to Daaliyah?" Esther asked.

Sheikh Solomon shook his head.

"I met her mother before I was married to Daaliyah," he said.

"That is disgraceful."

"I recently found out, and so I thought it was best if you all heard it from my mouth and not someone else," said Sheikh Solomon.

"Excuse me." Esther rose to her feet. She looked at Olivia with disgust on her face and walked out of the room. Daaliyah scurried after her.

"I think we should leave for a private talk," Joseph's father said to Sheikh Solomon. The two men rose to their feet and headed out of the room.

"That went well," Jacob said sarcastically.

"This is all your fault," Rania said to Olivia.

"You should have just returned when you said you would," said Marina. She sounded so irritated. Joseph knew it was because Marina did not accept Olivia as her sister, and she was annoyed at the fact that he wanted to marry Olivia instead. She shook her head and crossed her arms over her chest.

Chapter 12

"Olivia, how old are you?" Jasmine asked Olivia.

"Twenty-three," Olivia replied. Jasmine and Amir both raised their eyebrows.

"You are the same age as Jacob?" Jasmine asked. Olivia nodded. Amir looked at her with so much amusement on his face. She had noticed that both he and Jasmine were not surprised when Sheikh Solomon had dropped the news about Olivia's identity.

"I guess no one wants dessert," Amir joked.

"So, who are you?" Jasmine asked Daya.

"Oh, my name is Daya. I am Olivia's friend," Daya replied.

Rania rolled her eyes.

"She shouldn't be here either," Marina mumbled.

"Your father invited me to stay and he invited me to this lunch also."

"Well, you are not wanted," said Marina.

Olivia could feel another war of words about to commence. She touched Daya's arm and shook her head as a gesture for her to not say anything. She did not want to argue with her so-called sisters in the

Boutros's residence. She was still asking herself why she had come to this lunch. Olivia knew deep down that she wanted to get to know her father and have some kind of relationship with him. She knew that was the reason she had stayed and the reason she was at that miserably awkward lunch.

"Olivia, where are you from?" Jasmine asked.

"America, Atlanta," she replied.

Rania and Marina looked at each other. They stood up from the table.

"Where are you going?" Jacob asked.

"We would rather not share the table with her," Rania replied.

Jacob frowned.

"I understand that you do not like her, but you do not have to display this behavior in someone else's home," he said sternly.

Olivia was pleasantly surprised. Rania and Marina were behaving immaturely. Olivia was pleased that Jacob had called them out on it.

"It's alright," said Jasmine. "It's safe to say this lunch is over. We might as well all leave the table." Jasmine rose to her feet. Rania and Marina walked out.

"I am sorry about them," said Jacob as he stood up.

"Never mind it," Joseph replied.

Jacob nodded before he left the room. Amir rose to his feet. "Jasmine, we need to catch up," he said. Jasmine smiled.

"Yes, we do," she said with a mischievous look on her face. Jasmine touched Olivia's arm. "We should have lunch soon." Olivia smiled at her. She wondered if it was genuine offer. After seeing how Joseph's parents had to reacted to the news about her identity, she wondered if anyone in his family would be kind to her.

"No, you should not," Joseph spat out.

"Goodbye, Joseph." Jasmine and Amir left the room.

"So, you are Joseph," said Daya. She leaned back in her chair and just looked at him.

"I see you've heard about me," he said. He looked pleased, as if he was happy Olivia and Daya were speaking about him.

"I have."

"I am glad to hear that."

"You are quite handsome. I see why Rania and Marina are so into you," she said. Olivia crossed her eyebrows and looked at her. Daya was stroking his ego and she did not want that. He was already so conceited.

"What are you doing?" Olivia whispered.

"Thank you," said Joseph. He did not look grateful. He had a smug look on his face, as if he was saying "I know I am good looking."

"However, that means nothing here," said Daya. Olivia smiled a little. "Olivia will not be swayed by your looks or your money," she added.

Joseph grunted in response. He learned back in his chair and smiled a little. "Is that so?" he asked. He did not sound as though he believed her.

"Yes, it is so. You wanting to marry her is ludicrous. You know nothing about her. She will not agree just because you are a handsome sheikh."

"Daya, is it?"

"Yeah." Daya frowned.

"Are you the same age as Miss Grant?"

"Yes. Why are you asking about me?"

"He has a tendency to change the subject," Olivia pointed out.

"The two of you seem close," Joseph said to Daya. "So learning about Olivia's closest friend is a part of getting to know her."

"Okay then." Daya narrowed her gaze at him. "I hope that you do not have any ill intentions."

"What kind of ill intentions would I have?" Joseph asked.

"Joseph, you are interested in an American woman. She is unlike the women in this country."

"Elaborate."

"Stop treating her as though she is from here. She thinks differently and acts differently. She doesn't care about your prestigious family and power. That is not enough to win her over. So stop expecting her to come to you like every other woman you know and start courting her." Daya rose to her feet.

"My girl," Olivia whispered. She was pleased by Daya's little speech. As always, Daya had her back.

"Now if you'll excuse me, I'll go search for the restroom and give you two a moment to speak." Daya smiled and headed towards the door.

"Daya!" Olivia shouted after her. She did not want to be left alone with Joseph.

"She is feisty, just like you," Joseph said after Daya had left the room.

Olivia turned her attention to Joseph.

"I am feisty?" she asked.

Joseph nodded.

"We are finally alone," he said.

"Did you want us to be alone?" Olivia did not want that. She wanted to avoid him altogether.

"Of course. You owe me a dinner date," he said.

Olivia burst into laughter. It crazy to her that even after she had stood him up and refused his last offer, he still wanted to have dinner with her.

"This was an awkward lunch," said Olivia. It was her turn to change the subject.

"It really was."

"This is why I did not want to come."

"I am glad you came," Joseph spoke so gently. It made Olivia want to believe that he actually was glad that she came. "You look nice," he added.

"Because I am wearing a dress?" Olivia remembered him telling her to wear a dress at the mall.

"You listened to me." Joseph barely removed his gaze from Olivia. His gaze was intense. He looked so handsome and so attractive.

Olivia had to look away. She could not afford having any part of her fall for him.

"It was not about you. It was just appropriate," she said.

"Look at me," he demanded.

Olivia turned her head and looked at him.

"Why?" She frowned.

"I want you to look at me when you are talking to me," he ordered.

"You telling me what to do, that cannot happen. I will not stand for it," she said. She never liked being told what to do. Joseph did not respond immediately. He just kept staring at her with a smile on his face. It confused Olivia. She wanted to stand up and get out of the room. However, the smile on his face made her feel fuzzy on the inside.

"You are an interesting woman," said Joseph.

"I think it is time for me to leave." Olivia rose to her feet.

"We were still speaking."

"We spoke," she replied cheekily.

Joseph rose to his feet also. He placed his hand gently on Olivia's waist and kissed her on the cheek. Olivia jerked her head backwards. He had taken her by surprise. His large hand was sitting on her waist and it made her nervous.

"What are you doing?" she breathed.

"This is how we greet people or bid them farewell," Joseph replied in a tone that suggested that she had asked a dumb question. Joseph proceeded to kiss her other cheek. He pulled away and searched her eyes. "Until next time, Miss Grant," he said. He turned on his heel and headed out of the room.

Olivia placed her hand on her heart. She had felt so nervous. He made her nervous. Olivia felt her face warming up. She fanned herself with her hand. She wanted to slap herself for allowing him to make her perplexed. She cleared her throat and quickly left the room.

Chapter 13

As Joseph walked into the restaurant, people stared at him. The women smiled and greeted him. Joseph was used to that kind of attention. He just kept walking towards the back of the restaurant, where there was a room for VIP guests only.

"Good afternoon, Sheikh Boutros. Your guests have arrived," a neatly dressed waiter said to him.

"Okay," Joseph replied. The waiter opened the door for him. He walked into the modest sized air-conditioned room. The room had large windows that revealed a beautiful view of the beach. Joseph made his way to the table made out of the finest wood.

"Sheikh Solomon," Joseph said as he approached him.

Sheikh Solomon rose from his table and shook Joseph's hand.

"Thank you for coming," he said with a smile.

"Hello Olivia," said Joseph. Olivia was staring at Joseph in shock. He sat down opposite her. She whipped her head in her father's direction.

"I thought we were going to have lunch and talk," she said. She looked at Joseph. "Just the two of us," she emphasized.

"We talked." Sheikh Solomon smiled. "However, I have a meeting to attend."

Olivia narrowed her gaze at him. He smiled and walked away.

"I feel ambushed!" she called out after him. She looked at Joseph. "So, the two of you planned this."

"Not really," he said. Olivia frowned at him. "Eating with me will not kill you," he added.

Olivia smiled a little and picked up the menu.

"You are tenacious," she said to him.

"I want what I want and I get what I want."

Olivia looked up from her menu. "And you want me?" she asked, as if she did not know the answer to her question.

"Yes, I want you," Joseph replied.

Olivia put her menu down.

"I'll just have whatever you are having," she said. She leaned back in her chair and crossed her arms over her chest. "What is it about me that interests you?" she asked.

Joseph closed his menu and placed it on the table. He already knew what he wanted. He had been to the restaurant a few times.

"I think you are beautiful, and you have an attractive figure," he said. It was true. That and the fact that he had to get married within the next three months and he would rather it be to Olivia.

"So, you are just interested in my looks," she said. It surprised him a little. Most women would be so happy to hear a compliment from him. Olivia did not seem affected.

"Your body would look even better if you dressed properly," he said. She was wearing black harem trousers and a blue top. Her hair was tied up into a messy bun. Again, he would have preferred it if she wore a dress or a skirt.

"Excuse me?" Olivia did not look pleased by what he had just said. Before Olivia could say anything else, a waiter walked into the room.

"Are you ready to order?" he asked. Joseph nodded. The waiter reached into his pocket and pulled out a small notepad and a pen.

"Two portions of the roasted lamb, and make sure it's moderately spicy. Not too much and not too little," said Joseph. Olivia stared at him with her eyebrows crossed as he ordered. "I want the lamb with steamed vegetables and hummus on the side," he continued. The waiter nodded.

"What would you like to drink?" he asked.

"Bring me a jar of lemon water and Lebanese coffee. Bring me the coffee after the meal."

"Yes, sheikh." The waiter nodded and left the room.

"You could not even say please or thank you," Olivia said to Joseph after the waiter had left.

"It is his job to take my order," said Joseph.

Olivia shook her head.

"You didn't even order any carbs."

"Carbs?"

"Carbohydrates like rice, pasta or pita bread."

"It's best to not consume such foods."

Olivia narrowed her gaze at him. "Can we at least have ice cream or cake for dessert?" she said.

"No," he replied. He was a very healthy person. He went to great lengths to maintain his health and his physique.

"We are not even married and you are going to control what I eat?" she asked.

"You asked me to order for you."

"I know, but I did not think it meant no carbs." She sulked. She slumped her shoulders and pouted. Joseph wanted to smile. It the first time she had sulked in his presence. It was adorable.

"I'll buy you dessert next time," he said to her.

"Next time? How can you be so sure that there will be a next time?"

"There will." He was confident in his charms. He was going to melt her tough exterior by the end of the lunch. He was going to win her over, no matter what.

Moments later, the waiter returned with their food and placed it on the table. He asked if they needed anything else before he left. Joseph shook his head and waved his hand to dismiss him. The waiter left promptly.

"Well, it looks good," Olivia said as she picked up her cutlery. She cut into her appetizing lamb and took a bite. Joseph started eating also.

"What is your life like in Atlanta? What do you do?" he asked her.

"Now you want to get to know me," she replied sarcastically.

"I want to know what you so desperately want to return to."

Olivia smiled before she replied. "I've been working as a part-time receptionist for the past five years."

"Why part-time?" Joseph asked.

"I was in college, studying pharmacology."

Joseph raised his eyebrows. She studied science at a higher level. It was rare for him to meet a beautiful female scientist. Most beautiful women were into fashion and cosmetics. Olivia was a breath of fresh air.

"Now that you have graduated, you will be working in your field?" he asked.

She nodded.

"I would have been searching for jobs but instead I am here." She sighed.

"You can work here."

Olivia looked at him and narrowed her gaze. "Let's say that I agree to marry you. Then what?" she asked. Joseph looked into her hazel eyes and smiled. "I didn't say that I would agree, I am just trying to see where your head is," she quickly clarified. He already knew that it was hypothetical.

"Then we get married," he said.

"That's it?"

"Then your life would change for the better."

Olivia let out a laugh. She had an odd laugh. It was not feminine at all. "Don't you mean that your life would change for the better?" she said.

Joseph took a sip of his lemon water. He picked up a napkin and wiped his mouth.

The waiter returned for their plates. He carried them out and then returned with their coffee. Olivia picked up the small cup of coffee and studied it.

"It's so small," she said.

"It's very strong," Joseph informed her. She looked at him with a widened gaze.

"Really? How strong?"

"Taste it and find out."

Olivia took a sip. Her eyes flew open and she almost jumped out of her seat. "Wow!" she cried out.

Joseph laughed gently.

"I did warn you," he said.

"I like it." She giggled a little. He realized that she loved food. He had learned quite a bit about her over their lunch.

Joseph paid for their lunch after they were finished eating. He obviously was not going to let her pay for it. They walked out of the restaurant together. People stared at them as they made their way out. They gasped and whispered. Some people greeted him.

"I will drop you off at home," he said to Olivia as they stepped out into the hot weather.

"I would have said no if I had my own transport," she said. She shook her head. "I can't believe Sheikh Solomon tricked me like this," she added. Joseph smiled and gestured towards his car.

"You still call him Sheikh Solomon?" he asked her.

"What else would I call him?" she asked. She started fanning herself with her right hand. "It's very hot," she complained.

"Father."

"Why would I call him that?"

Joseph slid his hands into his pockets. "I guess it's too soon," he said to her. Joseph's driver got out of the car as they approached. He opened the backseat door. Joseph let Olivia get in first.

They kept talking about her father on their way to Sheikh Solomon's house. They talked about her awkward living arrangement. She was not getting along with her sisters or their mother. It was hard for her. She wanted to leave but her father really did not want her to. Joseph made a joke about her moving in with him, and she actually laughed. She was warming up to him. He had succeeded in melting her tough exterior.

Chapter 14

Olivia and Joseph arrived at Sheikh Solomon's residence. They parked right outside the house. Olivia had to admit to herself that having lunch with Joseph hadn't been so bad. Despite his vanity and arrogance, he was easy to talk to. He seemed to be a good listener also.

"Thanks for the lift," she said as she opened the door.

"No need to thank me. As your man, that's the least I could do," Joseph replied. Olivia's eyes opened wide. He had just referred to himself as *her* man. He had sounded so sexy when he said it. Olivia felt butterflies in her stomach.

"You are not my man," she said to him. "And I am certainly not your woman!"

Joseph smiled at her. He leaned towards her. This time Olivia quickly moved backwards. She moved too quickly and with so much force, she fell out of the car. She let out a squeak as she fell out. She landed on her bottom.

Olivia could not believe that she had just fallen out of the car like that. She had tried to dodge his kiss and ended up on her bottom. Joseph jerked his head forward and looked at her. "Are you okay?" he asked her. Olivia burst into laughter. She could not help but laugh at herself. Joseph raised his eyebrows.

"You find this amusing?" he asked her. Olivia laughed for a few more seconds before she cleared her throat and tried to compose herself.

"I am surprised that you don't," she replied. She sprang to her feet and wiped her bottom.

"I don't want you breaking anything."

"I'm okay, bye." Olivia headed into the house. She quickly rushed upstairs. She found Daya sitting on the sofas outside their bedrooms.

"You are here," said Daya. Olivia sat in the sofa opposite her.

"How are you?" she asked. Daya shrugged her shoulders.

"I need to go back to Atlanta."

Olivia sighed. "Me too," she replied. She really wanted to get out of that house but then if she returned, she would be leaving Sheikh Solomon behind.

"No, I mean I have to go back tomorrow," Daya replied.

"What happened?"

"My father has been admitted to the hospital again."

"Oh no." Olivia felt bad for Daya. Her father had bad kidneys. He had been waiting for a transplant for years. "We can leave early in the morning," she said. Daya shook her head.

"You have to stay here," said Daya.

"Why would I stay here when your father isn't feeling well?" Olivia knew Daya's father well. He had traveled a lot because of work when Daya was younger. However, he stopped because of his health. When he had time, he took Olivia and Daya for ice cream. It made Olivia wish she had a father also.

"You found out about your father in an unfortunate way. However, you know about his existence. You can't ignore him. You should stay here for a few more weeks and forge a relationship with him," Daya said.

"You came here with me. It's only right that I return with you and be there for you."

Daya smiled. "My father could die any day now but at least I would have no regrets. If Sheikh Solomon died tomorrow, you'd regret the time you threw away."

Olivia stood up and went to sit next to Daya. She threw her arms around her and embraced her tightly.

"Call me if anything happens. I will come in a heartbeat," she replied. "I am sure my future husband has a private jet I could borrow," she joked. Daya burst into laughter.

"I googled him actually," she said. Olivia released Daya from her embrace.

"You did?"

"Yes. It turns out his family is really rich, like filthy rich." Daya pulled her phone out of her pocket and tapped the screen a few times. "They have an oil company worth $1.2 billion."

Olivia's eyes opened wide.

"I am only worth five dollars," she said and burst into laughter. Daya laughed with her.

"I thought I would find something scandalous about him but I could not find anything. He's either a good man as your father says he is or he pays everyone to keep his secrets."

"Probably the latter explanation. I can't see a guy in his position having a squeaky clean record."

"You are right."

"Speaking of Joseph," said Olivia. She told Daya everything that had happened earlier. Daya buried her head in her hands before bursting into laughter.

"You cannot avoid him. Maybe he is your soulmate," she said. Olivia rose to her feet.

"I highly doubt it. We are not compatible and I am not complaining." She headed into her room.

***

The next morning, Olivia helped Daya pack her clothes and then escorted her to the airport. Sheikh Solomon had his driver take them.

Olivia and Daya walked into the airport with their arms linked. Olivia felt sad that Daya was leaving. It wasn't going to be easy without her. She was going to have to argue with her evil half-sisters by herself. She was also not going to be able to see Daya's father. She prayed that he would get a donor soon.

"Have a safe journey back," Olivia said to Daya.

"Have a safe stay here," Daya joked. "That house is like a battlefield."

Olivia laughed.

"It's Rania and Marina that need to be scared of me. I grew up in Atlanta, and you don't mess with a woman from the South," she said and smiled. Daya laughed.

"I know," she said and snapped her fingers. Daya and Olivia hugged once more. Daya went off to board her plane.

Olivia walked out of the airport. As she was heading towards Sheikh Solomon's car, she heard someone calling her name. She turned around and saw Jasmine. Olivia raised her eyebrows. Jasmine was the last person she expected to run into. Olivia smiled and waved.

Jasmine was much taller than Olivia. She was slim but her figure was curvy. She wore a pair of white trousers and a sky-blue blouse. Her long silky hair was not tied up. Jasmine was quite beautiful. She approached Olivia and stood in front of her. "Hello Olivia," she said.

"Hi, Jasmine," Olivia replied.

"Are you here to meet someone?"

"No. My friend was leaving for Atlanta."

"Daya?"

"You remember her name." Olivia smiled. Jasmine returned her smile.

"Are you in a rush?" she asked.

"No, why?"

"Let's have some coffee," Jasmine said and started walking into the airport. Olivia took a deep breath before she followed. She wondered why Jasmine wanted to have coffee with her. So far, none of the females that Olivia had met in Lebanon had been friendly to her.

Olivia and Jasmine went into a small café inside the airport. They ordered their coffee before they sat down. The café was nice. Each table was a different color. There were paintings hung on the wall. It was an interesting café.

"So, how are you?" Jasmine asked.

"I'm well. How are you?" Olivia was just waiting for Jasmine to tell her why she wanted to talk.

"I'm fine." Jasmine smiled. She took a sip of her coffee.

"Are you meeting someone?" Olivia attempted to make small talk.

"No, I am going back to Egypt."

"Do you live there?"

Jasmine smiled and shook her head. "I like traveling and doing volunteer work. I only came back because I wanted to see what you looked like," she said. Olivia's eyes widened.

"You wanted to see what I looked like?" she asked. Jasmine nodded.

"I already knew that Joseph wanted to marry you. I wanted to see what you looked like and I wanted to see what your character was like. Unfortunately, we haven't had time to get to know each other."

Olivia was surprised at the fact that Joseph had told her. "Are you his sister?" she asked.

"Cousin," she replied. Olivia nodded.

"And the other guy?"

"Amir, he's my twin."

"Oh I see." Olivia took a sip of her coffee. "I guess he knows about –" She stopped speaking. Jasmine nodded.

"Only Amir and I know about Joseph's interest in you."

Interest – Olivia would have phrased it differently. "I turned his offer down, did he tell you?" she asked.

"You did?" Jasmine looked shocked. "How come?" she asked.

"Shouldn't you know and love someone before you propose to them?"

Jasmine nodded. "I agree. It's just Joseph. No woman has ever turned him down," she replied. Olivia wanted to point out that he was not a god. It was possible for someone to turn him down.

"He is a handsome man. However, we met in the weirdest circumstances," she said politely.

"Please explain," said Jasmine.

"He was meant to choose between Rania and Marina but he ended up choosing me. I was not part of it. He shouldn't have chosen me."

"Now it's awkward between yourself and your sisters."

Sisters – she did not consider them to be her sisters. "It's more than awkward. We fight every day and it's just too much for me," said Olivia. Jasmine laughed a little.

"I understand. I don't want an arranged marriage either. I want to marry the man I love."

"Please explain that to Joseph," Olivia joked.

"You call him Joseph?"

"He told me not to but I still call him by his first name. Calling him Sheikh Boutros is just too long."

"And he lets you call him by his name?" Jasmine asked. Olivia nodded. She did not see the big deal. "Wow, he really does have a soft spot for you," Jasmine added.

"It's just his first name."

"It's different here. Since he is a sheikh, he must always be referred to by his title. Even I call him by his title when we are in public," she explained. Olivia didn't agree with the fuss but she said nothing more on the matter.

"I see," she said simply.

"He's a good guy. Once you get to know him, you will like him."

Olivia's subconscious screamed that she was already starting to like him but Olivia was not ready to admit to that yet. "I am sure he is," she replied. "But we are from different worlds. Even if I did agree to marry him, I do not think his mother would agree."

"Aunt Esther was not pleased when she found out about you," said Jasmine. "I am sorry that you had to witness that side of her."

"It's fine. I was not offended." It was true. Olivia was not offended. As long as she was not going to marry Joseph, she did not care what his parents thought of her.

"What do you do in Atlanta?" Jasmine asked. Olivia told her about her life back home. The two of them talked as they drank their coffee. Olivia was pleased that Jasmine was quite nice to her. It made her feel at ease.

The last call for the flight to Egypt was announced. Jasmine looked at her watch. "That's my flight," she said. Olivia nodded. They both rose to their feet.

"Have a safe journey," Olivia said to her. Jasmine quickly hugged her.

"We'll talk more when I return."

Olivia nodded with a smile. "Take care," she said.

Chapter 15

"I'm glad you decided to stay," Sheikh Solomon said to Olivia as they headed upstairs together.

"Your family won't be pleased," she replied.

"I hope that one day we will get to live happily together."

Olivia burst into laughter. "It's probably not going to happy anytime soon," she replied. Sheikh Solomon smiled.

"I had the maids prepare a room for you," he said.

"I have a room already." Olivia was confused. Sheikh Solomon shook his head.

"That was a guest room. This room will be yours." He led the way and Olivia followed. The room was not too far from her old room.

When they arrived, the maid opened the door for them. Sheikh Solomon let Olivia walk in first. The room was much bigger. The wooden walls were shiny and clean. There were large windows opposite her bed and there was a sitting area at the far end of the room. The room had its own bathroom. It was nice and clean. Olivia was impressed.

"Do you like it?" Sheikh Solomon nervously waited for her response. He looked like a schoolboy. Olivia could see that he desperately wanted her to like the room. He had probably put a lot of effort in getting the room fixed up for her.

"Yes, I do," Olivia said with a smile. She wasn't picky. The room was much bigger and nicer than her bedroom in Atlanta. "Thank you."

"I have one more thing for you." He searched his pockets and pulled out a small photograph and hand it to her.

"Mom?" She gasped when she saw the picture. It was a picture of her mother when she was younger. "You still had this?"

"I found it among my things."

Olivia looked at the sheikh and then at the photo. He still had a photo of her mother when she was younger. She could not believe that he still had a photo of her mother.

"When was this taken?" she asked looking at the photo. Her mother was wearing a T-shirt and baggy jeans. She had boots on. She had some oil smudges on her face and arms.

"We shared our first kiss after this photo was taken," he said. Olivia frowned.

"Ew, that was an image I did not need," she said. Sheikh Solomon started laughing.

Suddenly there was a knock on the door. A maid walked in with a house phone receiver. "Excuse me, Miss Olivia, you have a call," she said. Olivia crossed her eyebrows.

"Me?" she asked. "Who is it?"

"Sheikh Boutros."

Sheikh Solomon looked at Olivia with his eyebrows raised. "Are things advancing that fast between the two of you?" he asked.

"No!" Olivia protested. The maid handed her the phone.

"I will speak to you later." Sheikh Solomon happily left her to take the call. Olivia sighed and shook her head. The maid scurried out of the room and shut the door behind her.

"Sheikh Boutros," Olivia said into the phone. Joseph started laughing.

"Good evening, Miss Grant," he replied.

"Why are you calling me?"

"I can't call you?"

Olivia started walking towards her bed. "We have never called each other. Therefore, it's natural to assume that there was something urgent," she said as she threw herself onto her new bed. Fortunately, her suitcase had already been moved into her new room. So she did not have to go get it.

"The urgency is my need to see you," he replied. His voice sounded even deeper over the phone.

"We saw each other yesterday, not by choice, on my part anyway."

"That was more than twenty-four hours ago," he complained. Olivia laughed. She could not tell if he was genuine, creepy or just playing her. Her lack of experience with men made it hard for her to interpret the situation.

"I saw Jasmine at the airport today," she said.

"What were you doing at the airport?" he spat out.

"Relax, I was not trying to board the plane. I am not leaving yet. Daya was leaving."

"Oh." He sounded relieved. "Why was she leaving?"

Olivia told Joseph about Daya's father. Strangely she just told him as if she was used to telling him everything that happened in her life. Joseph listened to her and offered a few words of comfort. Olivia found herself thinking about what Jasmine had said about him – that was he was a good guy. Jacob and Sheikh Solomon had also said the same.

The topic changed from Daya's father to Olivia's childhood. They talked about where she grew up, petty fights she had, all her part-time jobs, how her mother worked two jobs. She opened up to him, even more than she had to her father.

"Tell me something about yourself," Olivia said to Joseph. They had barely spoken about him.

"Well." He paused for a moment. "I am out of town on business right now." It was not what Olivia wanted to know.

"What do you do?" she asked. She only knew that he was in the oil business but she did not know his role in the company.

"Before the drilling begins, all geology plans have to go through me. I have to inspect the oil rigs before drilling, during drilling and after. I have to meet with our clients and sell them the oil."

"That sounds like a lot of work."

"It is."

"Do you like your job?"

"I do."

"How old are you?"

"Twenty-nine."

She had assumed that he was twenty-eight. She was not far off. Olivia groaned as she rose from the bed. She peeled back the covers.

"What are you doing?" Joseph asked her.

"Getting into bed," she replied. She got into the bed and pulled the covers up to her waist.

"You can't be going to sleep already," he said. "We only just started speaking."

"I am not."

"I want to see you when I return from my trip."

"Oh that's nice," Olivia said sarcastically, even though she liked the fact that he wanted to see her. It made her smile.

"Olivia," Joseph said seductively. Her heart almost fell out of her chest.

"Yes, Joseph."

"When I can come back, come to my house for dinner."

"You are telling me to come, and not asking me?" she said.

Joseph laughed gently.

"I don't ask for things."

"Well, you better start now. That is if you want to see me." Olivia smiled and ran her hand through her hair. It was her first time teasing him and she liked it.

Joseph groaned in response.

"Can…" He stopped speaking, then tried again. "I want to see you… please," he said.

Olivia started giggling.

"Close enough," she replied. It was obviously hard for him but at least he was trying. It was funny.

"I'll send a car for you."

"When are you coming back?"

"On Thursday."

That was only a day and a half away. She had seen him on Sunday and Monday, and now she was going to see him on Thursday. She was seeing him a little too often.

"I am not going to wear a dress," Olivia said to Joseph before he could demand that she wear a dress. He had some kind of obsession with dresses.

Joseph laughed before he responded. "What do you have against dresses?"

"Nothing. I wear them at weddings and cocktail parties, not that I really go to cocktail parties but you catch my drift."

"You're a woman."

"And you're a man. Why are we stating the obvious?"

"You should dress accordingly."

"What is wrong with what I wear?" Olivia turned to lie on her stomach. The bed was nice and comfortable.

"You dress as though you do not care for yourself," Joseph replied. Olivia burst into laughter.

"It's not that bad," she said. Olivia was not bothered about wearing dresses and skirts but her clothes did not suggest that she did not care about herself. Joseph was just from a different world.

"My wife has to dress like a sophisticated woman."

"Boatneck dresses and pearls?"

"Exactly."

"Joseph, I'm twenty-three, not fifty-three."

"You would only need to dress like that when we are outside. When we are at home, you don't have to wear anything," he said in such a seductive tone.

"What?" Olivia snorted. "Don't start picturing me undressed."

"I was not but I am now."

"Your choice, but just to let you know I have cellulite and stretch marks." She lied to put him off. Granted her skin was not perfection just like any other normal woman but she did not have stretch marks.

"So what?" he replied.

"You don't mind cellulite and stretch marks?"

"No, I am not bothered."

Olivia was pleasantly surprised. She thought that he was the type of man to want a perfect woman with flawless skin. Suddenly the phone beeped. She looked at the receiver, it was low on battery. She gasped when she saw the time.

"What's wrong?" Joseph asked.

"I have been speaking to you for the past three hours." She had not even realized that she had been on the phone that long. Usually she could only speak to Daya for that long.

"Really?" Joseph was taken by surprise also.

"Yes and now I have to hang up. The phone is low on battery," she said.

"It still has battery. Speak to me until the battery has run out," he demanded as always. This time Olivia did not argue with him about the matter. She stayed on the phone until the battery ran out.

Chapter 16

Joseph yawned as he looked at the silver Rolex on his wrist. He was late for his meeting. He was to meet with some of the engineers working on the new oil rig. The elevator doors opened. He stepped out and headed down the hallway quickly.

"Good morning, Sheikh Boutros," one of the secretaries greeted him. Joseph crossed his eyebrows.

"Are you new?" he asked her.

"No, sir. I've been working here for six months."

"Hmm." Joseph opened the door and walked into the conference room. Amir and the other engineers were already sitting at the table. The engineers stood up and greeted Joseph. He dismissed them with his hand.

"Excuse my tardiness," he said to them as he sat at the head of the table. There was an oil geologist standing by the interactive white board. He was about to give a report.

"No worries, sheikh," said one of the engineers.

"Please begin," Amir said to the oil geologist. He nodded and started his report on the land. The engineers needed an estimation of how much oil they could get from the rig, and how deep they needed to drill.

As the presentation went on, Joseph's mind started drifting off. He started thinking about Olivia. He had never spoken to a woman for that long. He never had time and desire to entertain a woman for that long, especially one that he was not sleeping with. It was her fault that he was late to the meeting. He had stayed on the phone with her until 1 a.m. and then worked after he had finished speaking with her. He ended up sleeping longer than he intended.

"Joseph," Amir said. Joseph snapped out of his thoughts and turned his attention to Amir.

"Yes," Joseph replied. Amir raised his eyebrows.

"We need to change suppliers for the drilling machines."

"Of course."

The meeting finally ended. Joseph was glad that it was finished. He had not been paying attention at all. It was unlike him. He was always on the ball. Fortunately, Amir was there. He handled the meeting well.

"So what is on your mind?" Amir asked Joseph as they walked out of the conference office.

"Nothing," Joseph replied. Amir raised his eyebrows again. He did not look convinced. Joseph stopped walking. "I don't like these offices," he said randomly. They were at their offices outside Beirut. Joseph had not been there in months. He was suddenly realizing that the offices were poorly decorated.

"What is wrong with these offices?" Amir asked. He stopped walking and looked around.

"Those fluorescent lights look awful."

Amir looked at Joseph. "They look fine," he said.

"You! Come here," Joseph called out to the secretary that had spoken to him before the meeting. She rose from her desk and rushed over to Joseph.

"Yes, Sheikh Boutros," she said.

"These offices are appalling," he said. "Find someone who can repaint the walls."

"Yes, sir." She scribbled a few notes down.

"Change the lights, the blinds and this carpet. I want the carpet stripped off and replaced with wooden floors."

The secretary nodded and scribbled again. Amir shook his head. "You are fussy," he said.

"Our offices have to be up to par. It reflects on our reputation," Joseph replied. He turned his attention to the secretary. "Find out how much it would cost and send me the details. You will be in charge of the renovations. Make sure it gets done properly."

"Yes, sir," she replied. She looked a little bit intimidated. Joseph had just sprung such an important task on her.

"What is your name anyway?" Joseph asked her.

"Noor," she replied. Joseph nodded.

"I am counting on you, Noor."

Joseph nodded at Amir. The two of them walked towards the elevator. They had to go to an oil rig for inspection. A normal inspection included checking the progress of the drilling. Joseph was quite hands-on. He wanted to make sure that everything was done correctly.

***

Joseph returned from his business trip on Thursday night. He sent his driver to pick up Olivia. He then rushed upstairs and took a hot steamy shower. After he was finished showering, he stepped out of the large marble-tiled shower and quickly towel dried his thick hair.

He changed into a pair of beige chinos and a white polo shirt. He headed downstairs to the dining room where he waited for Olivia. His chef was already preparing their dinner. Of course Joseph had a chef. He appreciated food cooked to perfection.

Olivia arrived almost ten minutes later. One of his maids escorted her to the dining room. She wore a pair of high-waisted navy-blue jeans and a grey tank top, and grey pumps. Her wavy brown hair cascaded around her shoulders. She looked adorable.

"Good evening, Miss Grant." Joseph rose to his feet and approached Olivia.

"Hi Joseph," she replied. He gently wrapped an arm around her small waist. She had a small waist and wide hips. Joseph liked the way her body was shaped. It was hard for him not to touch her. He leaned in and kissed her on both cheeks.

"This time you did not try to run away," he said as he pulled away. When he tried to kiss her cheeks the last time he saw her, she tried to back away and ended up falling out of the car.

"I was too slow." Olivia smiled. Joseph pulled out the chair for her. "Thank you," she said as she sat down at the wooden table.

"Wine?" He gestured towards the wine bottle in the bucket of ice on the table. Olivia smiled and shook her head.

"I am not a drinker," she confessed. Joseph sat down at the head of the table. Olivia was sitting to his right. "Why are you sitting there? Why not opposite me?" she asked.

"This way I will be closer to you," he said. That and the fact that he was used to sitting at the head of the table. It befitted his position as a sheikh.

"How was your trip?"

"Productive."

A maid walked in and announced that dinner was ready. Two more maids walked in after her. They carried in trays of food. They placed the food on the table. Joseph reached out for the plate of oysters.

"I've never tasted oysters before," said Olivia. Joseph picked one up and used a small spoon to scoop some of the contents out.

"Here."

"Are you about to feed me?" Olivia raised her eyebrows.

"Just open up," he said. Olivia hesitated for a moment. Then she slowly opened her mouth. It was tantalizing being so close to her face. Her lips were nice and luscious. He suddenly wanted to kiss her. Joseph fed her and watched her taste it.

"It's an odd taste," she said. She crossed her eyebrows. "Fishy."

"Have another."

"I will feed myself this time," she said and picked up an oyster from the plate. Joseph smiled and nodded.

After they finished eating their oysters, they started on their dinner. Joseph felt amused as he watched Olivia eating. She enjoyed her food.

"Has your mother healed from the Sunday lunch?" Olivia asked Joseph.

"Healed from what?" he asked. Olivia swallowed before she spoke.

"From the shock of finding out that I am Sheikh Solomon's daughter."

"I have not spoken with her since then. I have been busy with work." Joseph sighed. He had been meaning to speak with her and his father also. He needed to tell them about marrying Olivia.

"That is another reason why we cannot marry," she said.

"What is?"

"Your mother. She would not accept me."

"Let me deal with that."

Olivia raised her eyebrows. Joseph reached out and touched her hand. She had such soft hands. He wondered if her lips were just as soft, and he intended to find out.

"I don't want a marriage that begins with me coming between a mother and her son," she said.

"She was in shock. She will come around after I speak to her."

"I want a marriage built on love, trust and friendship."

"We are friends right now, aren't we?"

Olivia burst into laughter. "No, we are not. We just know each other and have spent time together on a few occasions. That is all."

Joseph inched forward closer to her.

"I disagree. We more than just know each other." His voice was suddenly deep.

"Okay, I don't know you well enough to trust you."

"You do. You are just being difficult."

Olivia gasped and pulled her hand away from him. "I am not difficult," she protested. Joseph grabbed the leg of her chair and pulled it closer to him. Olivia gasped because of the sudden movement. "Are you that strong?" she asked.

"I am very strong." he replied matter-of-factly. He tugged on her tank top. "You shouldn't wear clothes like this. I can't have other men gawking at my woman." Olivia frowned at him.

"So we are going to talk about my clothes again." She sighed.

"You shouldn't frown at me."

"First of all, the only thing my top reveals is my arms. Secondly I am not your woman."

"You are mine. The sooner you come to terms with it the better."

Olivia's eyes widened. He knew she was about to protest his statement. He leaned closer to her until their faces were almost touching. "Joseph, what are you doing?" she asked.

"I am about to kiss you before you start complaining again," he said. She looked annoyed and nervous at the same time. He gently caressed her bare arm.

"Don't do that," she breathed. Joseph closed the gap between them and parted her lips with his. "Joseph," she whispered. He groaned in response. He kissed her slowly and gently. He kept his eyes open so that he could see her reaction as he kissed her.

Olivia put her hand on his chest and tried to push him away but she was not strong enough. She gave up after the second attempt and kissed him back. Her lips were just as soft as he thought they would be. She smelled good. Joseph really wanted to take her upstairs to his bedroom but he had to suppress the urge. He pulled away and stared at her for a moment. She opened her eyes slowly.

"Your kissing is not too bad but we can work on that," he said. Olivia pushed him away playfully.

"I am quite inexperienced on all things physical because I do not engage with every man that looks my way," she replied. She was so feisty and defensive. It was intriguing and attractive.

"I don't mind." He stroked her bottom lip with his index finger. He liked that she was innocent. It was refreshing. "I'd rather be the only man to fully have you." Joseph kissed her again, slowly and gently. Olivia wrapped her arm around his neck as she responded to his kiss.

"What is the meaning of this?" a voice full of shock spoke. Joseph and Olivia stopped kissing and looked towards the direction of the voice.

"Mother," said Joseph. His mother was standing in the doorway with a face as pale as a ghost.

Chapter 17

"Mrs. Boutros," said Olivia. She sprang up to her feet. She had not expected to see Joseph's mother. She had just walked in on Olivia kissing her son. Such bad timing. Olivia was enjoying the kiss. Joseph was such a good kisser. His lips felt good. His chest was as hard as stone. Olivia ran her hand through her hair.

"What are you doing here?" Esther asked Olivia.

"I invited her," said Joseph as he rose to his feet. He kissed his mother on the cheek. The elegantly dressed older woman did not look pleased.

Olivia noticed that Joseph's mother was tall. It made her more intimidating. She was dressed in black and white. Her clothes and her jewelry looked expensive enough to cover Olivia's yearly rent.

"Why?" Esther asked her son.

"For dinner," Joseph replied.

Esther looked at Olivia.

"I don't want you around my son," she said.

"That will be hard, since I want to marry her," Joseph responded.

Esther's facial expression changed from anger to shock. She looked like she was going to faint. Olivia whipped her head in Joseph's direction. She wanted to shout at him for telling her. She had already told him that she did not want to marry him. Now that he had told his mother, things were about to get more complicated.

"You what?" Esther spat out.

"I should leave," said Olivia. She did not want to be there for the fallout.

"Yes, please leave and go back to America."

"Mother!" Joseph exclaimed.

"I heard about you from Daaliyah. You are nothing but trouble."

Olivia was not surprised that Daaliyah spoke badly about her. That woman really did not like Olivia and it seems like she did not like her mother either. Olivia still needed to ask Sheikh Solomon how Daaliyah knew her mother. She could not believe that it had slipped her mind.

"Olivia has done nothing wrong," said Joseph.

"She has clearly succeeded in seducing you," said Esther.

Olivia almost burst into laughter. She could never successfully seduce anyone.

"I did not seduce your son," said Olivia.

"I was not talking to you."

"Mother, please stop being so rude. She is my guest," said Joseph. Olivia was pleasantly surprised that Joseph was defending her.

"She is a jezebel," said Esther. Jezebel? No one used that word anymore. Olivia certainly did not appreciate being called a jezebel. "Just like her mother," Esther added.

"Excuse me?" Olivia's temper instantly rose from zero to a hundred. "Please do not speak about my mother," she warned. She did not want to disrespect Mrs. Boutros in front of her son.

"She seduced Sheikh Solomon, did she not?"

"Mother, that is enough. You cannot speak ill of the dead," said Joseph.

"She did not seduce anyone and it's unkind of you to assume." Olivia was so angry and she knew she was not going to say anything nice to Mrs. Boutros. She turned her attention to Joseph. "Thank you for dinner but I have to go now," she said to him and stormed out of the room.

"Olivia!" Joseph called after her.

"Let her go," said Esther.

Olivia rushed out the front door. She was so angry she could punch something. She was willing to ignore almost anything Mrs. Boutros said but not when it came to her mother. That was crossing the line.

Joseph walked out the front door. He quickly approached Olivia. He touched her arm.

"Olivia," he said gently.

"She did not have to bring my mother into the conversation," she replied. She started tapping her foot on the ground. She did that when she was angry.

"I know. It was not necessary. I am sorry." Joseph gently rubbed her forearms. Olivia felt her eyes stinging. She blinked the tears away. She did not want to cry in front of Joseph. He searched her eyes.

"It's not your fault. You should go back inside," she said.

"Not until I am sure that you are okay."

"I am okay." Her voice shook. Joseph pulled her into his arms. Olivia just burst into tears. She placed her head on his shoulder and just cried. Joseph held her tightly and rubbed her back.

"It hasn't even been two months since she died," said Olivia between sobs. She cried for a few more minutes. Then she pulled out of Joseph's strong and warm embrace. "Sorry," she said. She had not planned on crying.

"Don't apologize," he replied. He wiped her tears off her cheeks with his thumb. He had taken her by surprise. He was being so gentle and comforting. It was nice.

"I am okay. You should go back in."

He held her waist tightly. "My driver will take you home. I will call you," he said.

"You do not need to check up on me."

"I do. You got upset while in my presence. I'll never let you get hurt in any way while in my care."

It was quite attractive how protective he was being. She was seeing a different side of him. It was quite appealing. Olivia touched his arm.

"Okay," she said and nodded.

Joseph walked her to the car and opened the door for her. He kissed her cheek before she got in. He shut the door behind her. "Take her home," he said to his driver.

***

"Great," Olivia mumbled as she walked through the front door. Daaliyah and her daughters were right by the stairs. Olivia tried to walk past them but Rania said something.

"Look who it is," she said.

"I can't believe she is still here," said Daaliyah. Olivia turned to face her.

"I expect this immaturity from your daughters but not you," Olivia said to Daaliyah. She was not in the mood for snarky comments because of Mrs. Boutros.

"What?" said Daaliyah.

"Did you just call my mother immature?" said Marina.

"I am tired of having to argue with the three of you every day," Olivia declared.

"Then leave."

"What is going on here?" said Sheikh Solomon as he walked through the front door. "This is getting old. Olivia is my daughter and she is not going anywhere. If you all can't get along, then don't speak to each other."

"This is my house too and I do not want her here," said Daaliyah.

"Is that why you have been talking badly about my mother and me to Mrs. Boutros?" said Olivia. Sheikh Solomon's eyes widened.

"You did what?" he said looking at his wife.

"You crossed the line this time." Olivia marched upstairs. She had had enough drama for the day. She rushed to her room and slammed the door behind her.

To her surprise, she heard a knock on the door moments later. "It's me," she heard Sheikh Solomon's voice.

"Come in," she called. He opened the door and walked into her bedroom. He sat down on the bed next to her.

"I thought things would have been better by now," he said.

"I should have just stayed at a hotel, but now that I am here, I will stay." She actually wanted to say that it was war. She was going to stay there just to piss them off.

"I am happy that you are here," Sheikh Solomon said gently.

"I've been meaning to ask, how does Daaliyah know my mother?"

Sheikh Solomon sighed before he responded, "When Ely and I were together, my mother did not approve. She arranged the marriage between Daaliyah and me."

"Oh, it was like that?" Olivia was surprised and intrigued at the same time. Sheikh Solomon nodded.

"Daaliyah and my mother were very close. So they basically did everything they could to break us apart."

"So my mother got sick of it all and decided to leave."

"I guess so," he said. Olivia started laughing. Sheikh Solomon looked at her as though she had gone mad. "What is funny?" he asked.

"You loved my mother and you still do, probably more than you love Daaliyah. That is why Daaliyah hates my mother and me so much," she said. Now that Joseph wanted to marry her and not either one of Daaliyah's daughters, it must be feeling like déjà vu for Daaliyah.

Chapter 18

"Joseph, what is wrong with you?" his mother questioned when he walked back into the dining room. "You still went after her after I told you not to."

"You did not need to bring up her mother. You crossed the line," he said to her. Esther took a few deep breaths to compose herself.

"You agreed to marry one of Sheikh Solomon's daughters."

"Olivia is one of his daughters."

"Joseph, don't play games with me."

"I am not playing games. I never play games," he replied.

"Why not Rania or Marina?" Esther asked.

"I am not attracted to either one of them." That was the truth. He was not attracted to them. The more he thought about it, the more he realized that they had awful personalities. Esther frowned at Joseph.

"Attraction? That is your excuse," she said. She shook her head. "Grow up!"

Joseph narrowed his gaze at her.

"I have made my decision and I will not change my mind," he said sternly. He respected his mother. However, he was not going to allow her to force him into marrying Rania or Marina.

"She is not even Lebanese!" Esther yelled out.

"She is half Lebanese and why does that matter?"

"I want full Arabic grandchildren."

"What about what I want?" he asked his mother. She was too concerned about what she wanted. It was starting to annoy him.

"What?" She looked confused.

"You wanted me to get married and I agreed. You wanted me to marry one of Sheikh Solomon's daughters and I agreed. At least let me choose which one."

"The illegitimate one?"

"Yes, that one."

"Your father is not going to be happy about this."

"I know but that will not change my mind," he said. Esther sighed loudly. She turned on her heel and left the room. Joseph had not planned on arguing with his mother when he told her about marrying Olivia but the situation had turned out differently. Esther had walked in on them kissing and so he had to tell her sooner. Then he had gotten annoyed at how she had spoken to Olivia.

Joseph let his mother leave. She needed to cool down. There was no reasoning with her when she was that angry. Joseph looked at his watch. Olivia should have been home by now, he thought to himself. He fished his phone out of his pocket. He called Sheikh Solomon's house phone and asked for Olivia. He headed upstairs as he waited for Olivia to get to the phone.

"Hello," said Olivia. Her alto voice was tantalizing.

"You're home," he said.

"No, I'm answering the house phone from the airport."

Joseph smiled as he walked into his bedroom. Olivia often used sarcasm. It was cute. "You okay?" he asked.

"I'm fine," she replied.

"What are you doing?"

"I was just talking to Sheikh Solomon."

"Father-daughter time?" Joseph sat on his bed and rested against the tufted headboard.

"Not really. I had a run-in with Daaliyah. So he came to see if I was okay," she replied.

"How bad was the argument?"

"We did not argue for too long because Sheikh Solomon walked in." Olivia sighed. "I am tired of the arguing. It's endless."

"Come live with me."

Olivia started laughing. "What?" she said.

"That kind of hostile environment is not good for you," he said.

"No it isn't, but living with you is not the answer."

"It is. You won't have to see your stepmother or your sisters on a daily basis." She would get to see him instead. However, Joseph was not serious about her moving in because he knew that she would refuse. In the past, she had refused simple things like having dinner with him. He just wanted to cheer her up a bit.

"That is true," she replied. "But then I would have to see you every day."

"You would like that."

"Living with you?" Olivia started laughing. "I think you are the one that would like living with me," she said. Joseph laughed gently in response.

Once again, Joseph found himself speaking to Olivia for hours. It was oddly easy to speak to her. It was new to him. He had never had the time nor the patience to speak to anyone for more than ten minutes.

***

Sheikh Boutros senior called his son for breakfast at his house. Joseph was not surprised that his father had summoned him. Obviously his mother had told him about their heated disagreement over Olivia. Joseph straightened his tie before he walked into the dining room.

"Good morning, Father," Joseph said as he walked into the room. His father was sitting at the table. The maids had already set the table.

"Good morning," his father replied. Joseph joined him at the table. He picked up the coffeepot and poured himself a cup of coffee.

"Where is mother?"

"She is upstairs. She is still not ready to see you."

For once, Joseph felt like rolling his eyes. He hated it when Olivia did it. It was rude. She needed to be tamed a little.

"She should not be upset," Joseph replied. He had not done anything to upset her.

"She just found out that her only son wants to marry a non-Arabic woman, an illegitimate child," said his father.

"She is half Arabic."

"Half," his father emphasized.

"She wanted me to marry one of Sheikh Solomon's daughters and that is what I am going to do," Joseph replied.

His father raised his eyebrows.

"Olivia is a beautiful girl but I am not sure that she is right for you."

"Neither is Rania nor Marina," Joseph pointed out. The two of them were right on paper but in person it would not work. Granted he did not know much about them but he saw the way they acted around him and how they treated Olivia. It was enough to put him off.

"What is wrong about the two of them?"

"I am not attracted to either one of them. I have seen how they carry themselves and I am not impressed."

His father barely reacted. He just ate his eggs and swallowed. "It's your choice," he said. "However, you know that if you are not married by the time you are thirty, then I will recruit someone else."

Joseph was irritated by the ultimatum. He was their only child and therefore, he should inherit the company.

"Who else would you pick?" Joseph asked. "You would give the company to a stranger?"

"There are options."

"This is not right. I have worked in this company for fifteen years." Joseph had started working for his father when he was fourteen years old. He started by being an errand boy and then graduated to doing small administrative duties such as filing. He worked at Boutros Oil during his studies at the university. He knew the company very well and he felt that he deserved to inherit it.

"I don't question your work ethic. However, you need to settle down. Having a different woman every other week is detrimental to our reputation."

"I have always been discreet about my personal life." Joseph was quite particular about the women he invited into his personal life. He never wanted to have scandals or anything from his personal life affect his work life.

"You should have a family of your own by now," said his father.

"You and mother both wanted me to settle down and I have agreed. Surely I should be able to pick my own wife," said Joseph.

"Can you not change your mind on this?"

"No."

His father was silent for a moment. "Your mother will not agree to this easily," he said.

"I am aware." Joseph could see his father starting to change his mind.

"I will need to sit down with Olivia. I need to see what kind of a woman she is."

Joseph nodded. "Naturally," he said. Now he just needed to convince Olivia to sit down with his father. Knowing her, she would put up a fight and say that she was not going to marry him.

Joseph really needed this to work. He needed to get married soon in order to gain full control of Boutros Oil Ltd. As much as he did not want to admit it to himself, he was also starting to care for Olivia. Seeing her crying had changed something within him. He was not happy seeing her cry. He especially loathed the fact that she was crying because of his mother. He was not going to allow any member of his family to upset her like that ever again.

"Have you talked to Sheikh Solomon about this?" his father asked.

Joseph nodded. "I have," Joseph said.

"What did he say about this?"

"He was shocked as well but since I was not going to change my mind, he just accepted it."

"He has not mentioned anything to me."

"I wanted to tell you myself, after he had told you about Olivia being his daughter." Joseph was going to tell them after they had gotten over the news of Olivia being Sheikh Solomon's daughter. However, things had not worked out that way.

"I have to go to work." Joseph wiped his mouth with a napkin. His father nodded.

"Tell Olivia that I want to meet with her on Sunday for lunch."

"So soon?" He was not sure that she was going to agree.

"Why waste time?" his father asked.

"No reason." Joseph rose from his chair. "I will take my leave now," he said. He buttoned up his suit jacket and then he headed out.

Chapter 19

"What's up, kid?" said Jacob as he walked out of the house. Olivia was sitting on the grass in the garden soaking up some sun. She looked up and smiled at Jacob.

"I haven't seen you a few days. Where have you been?" she asked.

"I was in Qatar."

"Business?"

"Pleasure." Jacob smiled as though he had some naughty secret. Olivia stretched her arms out to him.

"Help me up," she said. He looked at her as though she was crazy.

"You are not that old. You can get up on your own," he said. Olivia pouted and helped herself up.

"So what kind of pleasure took you to Qatar?" She did not know much about Qatar or any other Middle Eastern country. She had never gotten the opportunity to travel.

"There was a fashion show." Jacob started walking. He gestured for Olivia to follow. She followed.

"You're into fashion?" Olivia asked.

"Not really. Just someone invited me."

"That woman you keep messaging?"

Jacob smiled and did not respond. Olivia nudged him playfully. "Jacob has a girlfriend," she teased. Jacob started laughing.

"Far from it," he said.

As they were walking, Olivia could hear voices getting louder and louder. She could tell that one of them belonged to Daaliyah.

"I feel bad for you," the other person said to Daaliyah.

"Me too." Daaliyah replied. "The moment I found out that Elizabeth was pregnant, I wanted her to go before he found out."

Olivia and Jacob looked at each other.

"What did you do?" the other person asked.

"His mother and I told her to leave. We made it clear that she was never going to be accepted into the family. We offered her money but she refused." Daaliyah laughed a little.

"How about Jacob, when were you pregnant with him?"

"Just as my mother-in-law suggested, I got the sheikh drunk and slept with him. So when Elizabeth left and he was threatening to give up the company to follow her, I told him that I was pregnant. So he had to take responsibility."

Olivia and Jacob turned a corner. They saw Daaliyah sitting at the table in the garden with Esther.

"Mother!" Jacob spat out. His face was stained in shock. Olivia was also shocked at what she had just heard. She knew Daaliyah was evil but Sheikh Solomon's mother as well? She felt angry knowing that Daaliyah and her mother-in-law had conspired to get rid of Elizabeth.

"Jacob." Daaliyah gasped as she rose to her feet.

"That was how I was conceived?" Jacob looked disgusted. "Even before you and dad were married?"

And you thought my mother was the jezebel, Olivia thought to herself. She decided to keep her words to herself. It was enough that Daaliyah had just outed herself in front of her son. Olivia just walked off without saying a word.

She went to look for the driver and asked him to take her to Joseph's house. She did not know anyone else and she did not feel like staying home. She just wanted to get out of the house. She soon arrived at Joseph's house. Olivia got out of the car and walked up the concrete steps leading to his front door. The maid opened the door for her.

"Is the sheikh home?" Olivia asked. She instantly chastised herself for saying the sheikh. She never called him by his title.

"He is in his office," the maid replied.

"On a Saturday?"

"He works during the weekends."

The maid escorted Olivia to Joseph's office. His office was somewhere downstairs. Olivia was not sure she could find her way back to the front door. Joseph's house was quite big. It was as if she was in a hotel.

The maid stopped in front of French double doors and knocked before she walked in. Joseph was sitting at his desk looking at some paperwork.

"I am sorry to disturb you. Miss Olivia is here to see you," the maid said to Joseph so gently as if she was scared to be scolded for disturbing him. Joseph whipped his head in her direction in shock.

"Olivia," he breathed. The maid scurried out of the room and shut the doors. Olivia walked into the grey and white office. It was so neat, and beautifully decorated. She walked over to the desk and sat in a white tufted chair in front of it.

"Hi," she said. Joseph put his pen down and started packing up his paperwork.

"What are you doing here?" he asked her.

Olivia slumped her shoulders.

"Unfortunately, I do not know anyone else nor do I have anywhere else to go," she said. She knew it sounded rather rude, as though he was the last person she wanted to see. However, that was not the fact. It was true that she did not know anyone else but she wanted to see Joseph. He was the first person she thought of but she was not going to tell him that.

"What happened?" he asked her as he shoved his paperwork into the drawer of the desk.

"Your mother came over."

"Oh." He looked disappointed.

"Don't worry, she did not do anything to me," Olivia clarified. "It was Daaliyah. I heard her telling your mother that she and her mother-in-law made my mother leave Sheikh Solomon. They tried to pay her to leave but she refused the money."

Joseph looked stunned. He was clearly in shock. Olivia told Joseph everything she had heard.

"It's shocking for me to hear because I grew up knowing Daaliyah," said Joseph.

"I was dying to find out why Sheikh Solomon didn't know about me and why he broke up with my mom," said Olivia.

"Are you okay?"

Olivia nodded. "I feel disgusted by Daaliyah, and I feel guilty towards the sheikh," she said.

"Why do you feel guilty?" Joseph asked.

"I did not want to have anything to do with him. I was angry at him for not looking for me. Now I see that it was all Daaliyah's fault." Olivia ran her hand through her hair.

"Don't feel guilty. You did not know."

"Why are you working over the weekend?" Olivia did not want to keep speaking about Daaliyah.

"I always work during the weekend," he replied.

"You are such a boring man."

"Excuse me?"

"Normal people do something fun over the weekend."

"What is fun to you?"

"Trying out new dishes, swimming, movies, binge watching television shows." Olivia sighed. She could think of so many other things that she would rather do than working.

"I have a swimming pool," said Joseph.

Olivia raised an eyebrow. "Do you expect me to swim now?"

"If you want to."

Olivia burst out laughing. "I don't have a bathing suit," she said.

"Don't you swim in a bikini?" Joseph asked.

Olivia shook her head. "No. I like to wear a one-piece swimsuit."

"Like a ten-year-old?" Joseph started laughing.

"Why is that funny, Joseph? There plenty of women my age that wear one-pieces!" she defended herself. Daya often laughed at her also for not wearing bikinis.

"I am sure there are," he said sarcastically.

Olivia crossed her arms over her chest in an attempt to sulk. However, she quickly abandoned the sulking. "I feel hungry," she said. She was always hungry.

"What would you like to eat?" Joseph asked. "I'll let my chef know."

"You have a chef?" It was still hard for her to comprehend how rich he was. She had never been around someone with a bank balance more than five hundred dollars.

"Yes," he replied. Olivia did not even know why she had asked him. He had a mansion the size of a hotel and a lot of maids. Of course he had a chef.

"Never mind, I will go cook myself." Her boldness surprised herself. She was actually about to cook in Joseph's house.

He raised his eyebrows. "You can cook?"

"Why does that surprise you?"

"Not many women I've met can or want to cook."

Olivia rolled her eyes.

"I am sure that I am nothing like the women you've met," she said. She was convinced that he only had relationships with tall models. Olivia sprang to her feet.

"You are right. No woman would ever come to my house dressed like that," he said eyeing Olivia up. She was wearing a loose-fitting shorts and a loose-fitting basketball T-shirt.

"Maybe they should. Women are too caught up in trying to look good all the time. That means nothing if you have a rotten personality," she said. Joseph smiled as he rose to his feet.

The two of them left his office and headed to the kitchen. Joseph dismissed all the staff from the kitchen and dining room per Olivia's request. She did not mind cooking and cleaning by herself. So she thought it would be nice if Joseph gave them the afternoon off.

Olivia gaped at the kitchen when she walked in. The kitchen was huge. It had marble counters and floors. The stove had ten burners and a massive oven beneath it. The fridge was like a slice of heaven. It was a large cold room with all kinds of food. There was enough to last her two months.

Joseph sat on a high stool with a black leather seat and silver legs. He crossed his arms over his chest and watched Olivia finding her way around the kitchen. She took out the pots and utensils she needed and placed them on the counter. She went back to the cold room and retrieved steak, peppers, cheese, lettuce, mayonnaise, cucumbers and tomatoes.

"Cheese?" Joseph questioned.

"You'll see why later," Olivia replied.

"It's my first time coming in here."

Olivia's eyes widened. "Your first time in your own kitchen?" she asked in shock.

Joseph shrugged his shoulders.

"Yes. I have no reason to come in here."

Olivia shook her head. He was so spoiled. How could someone not enter the kitchen in their own house? His maids probably did everything for him. Olivia washed her hands and then started marinating the steak.

"My father wants to have lunch with you," said Joseph. Olivia looked up. She could not believe what her ears had just heard.

Chapter 20

"What?" Olivia said. She stared at him with her hazel eyes widened. She was clearly shocked.

"My father wants to have lunch with you," Joseph said. He knew that she was going to say no, however, he really needed her to agree. Joseph wanted Olivia to sit down with his father. If he liked her, then maybe he would try to convince his mother into agreeing with the marriage.

"Why?" Olivia raised an eyebrow. She looked as though she was suspicious about something.

"He wants to feel you out; see what kind of a person you are." That was putting it lightly. His father was a very intimidating man.

"Why though?" Olivia stopped marinating the steak, suddenly realizing the answer to her own question. "He knows that you want to marry me."

"Yes," Joseph said simply.

"Oh my gosh!"

"Of course I told him. Everyone knows now." Joseph smiled mischievously.

"How disappointed they will be to find out that I won't marry you," she said sarcastically. Joseph smiled. "When does he want to meet with me?" she asked.

"Tomorrow," he said.

"So soon?"

"Yes."

Olivia sighed very loudly. "Where?" she asked.

"At restaurant," he said. Olivia nodded.

"It's better that way. If we met at his home, that would be bad because I would run into your mother," she said. Joseph slightly crossed his eyebrows. He thought that she would refuse and get angry about it. Strangely she had agreed so easily.

"Okay then," he said.

Joseph sat on his stool and watched Olivia cooking. He was so fascinated by her. She was walking around his kitchen and cooking so comfortably. It was as if it was her kitchen. Joseph had never had a woman cook for him. In fact, all of the women he had been in relationships with did not like cooking. They loved the fact that he had a chef and maids. They liked being pampered.

"You're making rice?" Joseph asked as Olivia poured rice into the rice cooker.

"Of course I am," she replied. "Carbs!" She grinned at him. She washed the rice before she cooked it. Then she prepared a salad.

"So the cheese is for the salad," said Joseph.

"Yes." Olivia put in a teaspoon of sugar. Joseph's eyes flew open.

"Sugar?" he questioned. Olivia started laughing.

"Relax. It tastes good," she said.

"Wow." He was in shock.

"You have never even seen your food getting prepared."

"That is true."

Olivia finished cooking a while later. She served Joseph with the well-grilled steak, rice and salad. Joseph had to admit, the food looked quite appetizing. They sat on the stools at the island counter of the kitchen.

"Thank you," Joseph said to Olivia when she handed him his plate and a knife and fork.

"You're welcome." Olivia sat down with her plate. "I'm so hungry." She dove into her food.

"This is an unhealthy meal," Joseph pointed out. There was mayonnaise and cheese and white rice. He liked his meals strictly healthy.

"Well." Olivia was looking at Joseph waiting to hear what he thought of the food. Her big hazel eyes filled with so much expectation stared at him. She was so adorable.

"It surprisingly tastes good," he said honestly. The food did taste good. She could give his chef a run for his money.

"Of course it does. I told you that I can cook," Olivia gloated.

"Where did you learn how to cook?"

"My mother. She was a great cook."

"What was she like?"

"Very feisty but soft-hearted."

"So that's where you got it from." Joseph smiled. Olivia smiled and rolled her eyes.

"Joseph, I am not really that feisty," she said to him. He raised an eyebrow as he chewed. Olivia burst into laughter. "Whatever," she said.

After they were finished eating, Olivia cleared the dishes and started washing them. He tried to stop her from washing up but she refused. She said that she could not leave the dirty dishes for someone else.

"I should go," she said when she was finished cleaning.

"So soon," said Joseph. He did not want her to go just yet.

"I have been here for hours." Olivia walked towards him. He grabbed her hand and pulled her closer to him. "Joseph!" she cried out. He positioned her between his thighs and wrapped his arms around her. She fit perfectly in his arms. His head was buried in her neck. He inhaled her sweet scent and held her so tightly.

"Joseph what are you doing?" Olivia screamed and laughed as she tried to push him off. Joseph laughed with her and held her tighter. "It's pointless, I am not strong enough." She stopped trying to fight him off.

"It's going to be the same thing with our marriage," Joseph said.

"What do you mean?"

"Eventually, you are going to stop fighting me on the matter and you will agree to marry me."

Olivia laughed. "Your mother wouldn't attend the wedding. My sisters would probably assassinate me during the wedding," she said. Joseph laughed gently.

"Is this you agreeing to marry me?"

"This is me reminding you that it is a bad idea."

"It's not." Joseph caressed her lower back. He wanted to touch her and kiss her. Olivia flinched and let out a squeak.

"Don't do that!" she cried out.

"Are you ticklish?"

"I am." Olivia managed to wiggle out of his embrace and jumped a few steps back. She fanned herself with her hand. "I need to sort things out back in Atlanta," she said.

"Like what?" he asked.

"I need to go back. I took my annual leave to come here and I've called them twice to extend it, which they were not happy about."

"You can just send them your resignation. You don't need to worry about work when you are with me."

Olivia raised her eyebrows and shoved her hands in her pockets. "And be a housewife? No way," she said.

"What is wrong with that?" he asked. He agreed with the idea of a man providing anything and everything for his woman. Even though he had never wanted to get married, he always provided for the woman that he was in a relationship with.

"Everything. Some women are okay with it but I am not. I like being independent. I certainly did not go to college just to be a housewife."

"I just don't want you to worry about work and rent."

"Thank you but I want to work. I like the satisfaction of hard work and being able to buy things for myself. I don't want to rely on anyone."

Joseph nodded. She continued to shock him. Women would ask him to buy them things. Olivia actually wanted to work and provide for herself. He was impressed by her, as usual.

"What happens if you get fired from this job?" he asked her.

"That will be really awful. Fortunately, I have some savings and I am ahead of my rent by two months."

"You are quite responsible."

"My mother and I have been through a lot. So I learned how to always be prepared for the worst."

"I wish I had had the opportunity to meet her."

"You would have liked her."

"If she was anything like you, then I would have really liked her," he said. Olivia shyly tucked a wavy lock of hair behind her ear. It was so amusing to Joseph because she was such a feisty person but she also got shy. He caught her on many occasions trying to hide it but he knew that she was shy or that he was making her nervous. He could spot little changes in emotions and demeanor.

Chapter 21

"Show me what you are wearing," Daya said through Skype. Olivia had video called on Skype. She had a lot to tell her. After she had made sure that Daya and her father were okay, Olivia told Daya everything that had happened since she left.

"I am wearing this white peplum dress," Olivia said as she rushed towards her laptop. She twirled to make sure Daya could see the entire outfit.

"That is decent," said Daya.

"It is. I am so nervous, Daya. I hope his father isn't as mean as his wife."

"If you marry Joseph, you will have a monster for a mother-in-law." Daya burst into laughter.

"Why would I marry Joseph?" Olivia asked. The idea was no longer strange or bad to her. Joseph was easy to talk to. She enjoyed talking to him about anything. He was the only man that she had ever been so close to, especially in such a short time.

"It seems as though your relationship has advanced," said Daya. Olivia sighed deeply.

"Why does everything have to be so complicated?"

"That's life, my darling."

Olivia slipped into her white flats. She had her hair neatly packed into a tight bun. She wanted to look as presentable as possible. For some odd reason, she wanted to make a good impression on Joseph's father.

"Why couldn't Joseph ask for a relationship? Why marriage? It's so final. I thought that by now he would have abandoned the idea," said Olivia.

"Maybe he genuinely likes you. At the start I was wary of him but now that you've told me about how he stood up for you in front of his mother and comforted you, I am starting to change my mind," said Daya.

"You and me both." Olivia picked up her laptop. "I have to go now. I can't be late," she said.

"Okay, good luck."

"Thanks." Olivia ended the call. She put the laptop on the nightstand and rushed out of the room.

***

Olivia arrived at the restaurant a while later. The restaurant was empty when she arrived. She stood at the entrance gaping at the big room. It had a black and maroon décor. A waiter dressed in black approached her.

"Good afternoon, miss," he greeted her.

"Hi, is the restaurant open?" she asked as she looked around.

"What is your name?"

"Olivia," she said skeptically.

"The sheikh will be here soon. Please have a seat." He gestured towards a reddish wooden table in the middle of the room. She slowly walked towards the table. She pulled out a chair for herself and sat down.

"Would you like some water or anything while you wait for Sheikh Boutros?" the waiter asked Olivia.

"Yes, some water, please." She needed some water to cool her nerves. The waiter nodded and disappeared. He reappeared with a jar of water and a glass a few moments later. He placed the glass on the table and poured out some water for Olivia. She drank her water as she waited.

The sheikh arrived moments later. He was dressed in a charcoal grey suit. He was tall, taller than Sheikh Solomon. The sheikh looked very much like Joseph, an older version of him. He had a lot of grey in his hair. Olivia put her glass down and rose to her feet.

"Good afternoon, Miss Grant," Joseph's father said as he approached Olivia. She felt odd hearing him calling her Miss Grant. Joseph always called her that.

"Good afternoon," she replied. She extended her hand and gestured for a handshake. He took her hand into his and shook it. He had a firm grip. He gestured towards the chair for Olivia to sit down. She nodded and took her seat.

"Thank you for agreeing to meet me," he said to her.

"It's okay." Olivia laughed nervously. She did not feel like she had a choice. That's when it dawned on her. The restaurant had been closed down so that they could dine alone. She partially wished that there were other people around. Joseph had offered to come with her, but as much as she wanted to say yes, it was not wise. She needed to see his father alone.

"I have already instructed them on what to serve us. I hope that is okay with you," he said.

"It's fine." She could eat almost anything. He smiled and nodded.

"What do you do in America?"

Olivia told him about her part-time job as a receptionist and the fact that she had just finished her pharmacology studies. There wasn't much more she could tell him. She was not an interesting girl. Her life was plain and simple.

The waiter brought out their food. Olivia normally drooled over food. However, today she couldn't focus on it. She was just waiting for Joseph's father to bring up the marriage thing. That was the reason why he had called her.

"I like my food nice and simple. I do not like overcomplicated meals that have an extravagant appearance but lack in taste. It's as if the chef is trying to cover up the fact that his food tastes badly," said Joseph's father.

"Simple is good," Olivia replied. She was sure that there was a threat somewhere in Joseph's father's words. They were about food but they made her uneasy. Sheikh Boutros senior was a little bit more intimidating than his son. He cut through his lamb so easily and then put the piece of the meat in his mouth. He chewed slowly without taking his eyes off Olivia. Unlike his son, he had eyes as dark as midnight.

"Just like people. I like people that are transparent and honest. I hate pretentious characters," he said.

"So do I," said Olivia. "I value integrity and modesty." Just like the sheikh, she did not like pretentious characters.

"Good. I see that we are on the same page," he said. He took a sip of his drink. "My son wishes to marry you. What's your position on this matter?" he asked. Ahh, at last, Olivia thought to herself. He finally spoke about the marriage.

"I feel that it is still too early for us to get married," she said. She would rather it was Joseph that told his father that they were not getting married. That and the fact that she did not think it was such a bad idea that Joseph was interested in her.

"That is correct. However, you must know that you and my son are not a match," he said frankly.

"Only if we are comparing our financial status," she said boldly. She was not about to sit there and be told that she was not good enough for Joseph.

"Please elaborate," he said with so much fascination on his face.

"I don't think it's fair for anyone to say that we cannot be together just because I am not all Arabic or because I am an illegitimate child."

"No, it is not fair. However, that is life. Life isn't fair."

"We don't choose to be born in rich families or poor families."

The sheikh nodded. "If you and my son were to marry, what could you offer him?" he asked. Was he so jaded that he believed that marriages should be considered as alliances for financial gain? Olivia asked herself.

"Love." The word left her mouth before she could stop it. Was she really prepared to love him? "Loyalty, respect, honesty and unwavering support," she added. Sheikh Boutros senior raised his eyebrows. He was clearly surprised.

"Those are fine qualities but not for a man like Joseph. He needs a woman with a good background. A woman that can contribute to his position. I need my son to marry a woman from a powerful family," he said. Olivia almost laughed at the greed. Money and power. Was that all that mattered?

"He has enough money and power," she said to him. "But does he have enough happiness?"

"Proceed with caution," Sheikh Boutros senior warned.

"They say a king is very lonely," she said. "He has everything and yet there is no one he can trust."

"You are saying my son is lonely?"

"I am saying that he could be. Money doesn't buy happiness."

"Do you know my son enough to know what makes him happy?" he asked after a moment. That was a good question, Olivia thought to herself.

"I would like the opportunity to get know him and find out what makes him happy," she replied. The sheikh laughed a little. He picked up a maroon napkin and wiped his mouth and hands.

"You are an intriguing woman," he said. Olivia smiled in response. She hoped that it was a compliment. "You are different from your father," he added.

"I hope that is a good thing," Olivia replied.

"Only time will tell." Sheikh Boutros senior looked at his watch. "I must bid you farewell. I have a meeting to attend," he said as he rose to his feet. Olivia also stood up.

"Thank you for the lunch," she said to him.

"Do you have transportation? "

"Yes I do." Olivia smiled. The sheikh smiled. He turned on his heel and left the room. Olivia placed her hand on her heart and sighed with relief. Joseph's father was an intimidating man. She had managed to stay calm in his presence but it was hard. He was different from his wife. She shouted and said nasty words. However, Joseph's father was calm and scary.

Chapter 22

After Olivia was finished having lunch with Joseph's father, Jacob picked her up from the restaurant. The two of them had plans. They had a place they needed to go to. She felt nervous about it because she did not know what to expect.

"Are you ready?" Jacob asked when they had arrived at their destination. Olivia looked out of the window. They were parked outside a beautiful villa outside Beirut.

"I am," she replied.

"Okay."

Jacob and Olivia got out of the car. They walked towards the villa. Jacob fished a key out of his pocket and unlocked the door. They walked in. The interior was amazing. There were clean stone floors and high ceilings. A maid walked out of a room and into the corridor.

"Jacob, hello," she greeted him.

"Hello," he greeted her and kept walking. He took a left turn and walked into a room. Olivia followed. The room was nicely furnished with rare and expensive-looking furniture. There was an elderly lady sitting at the chairs reading a book. She was wearing a long-sleeved sky blue dress and an expensive-looking necklace. She had her grey hair pinned up into a fancy-looking bun. She looked up when Jacob and Olivia walked in.

"Jacob!" she gasped. She put her book down immediately.

"Hi, Grandma," he said as he approached her. He kissed her on both cheeks.

"This is a nice surprise." She turned her attention to Olivia. "Who is she?" she asked.

"This is Olivia, your granddaughter," said Jacob. Her eyes widened.

"What?" She laughed a little. "What are you talking about?" she asked. Jacob looked at Olivia and gestured for her to sit down. The two of them sat down at the sofas.

"My name is Olivia Grant and I am Elizabeth Grant's daughter," said Olivia. Jacob's grandmother's smile disappeared. Her face immediately turned pale. She placed her hand on her heart and started blinking rapidly. She closed her eyes and shook her head repeatedly.

"Elizabeth's daughter?" she asked.

"Yes." Olivia nodded. She felt weird about being there. Jacob had come up with the idea to go see their grandmother. He was cross with her for what she had done.

"Does your father know about her?" she asked Jacob.

"He does. We have all known for the past three weeks," he replied.

It was crazy to Olivia that she had been in Lebanon for three weeks. It felt as though she had been there for much longer. Too much had happened. Her life had completely changed and there was nothing she could do about that.

"Why did nobody tell me?" their grandmother asked.

"Yesterday, I learned that you knew about Elizabeth's pregnancy and you purposely kept it from father." Jacob ignored her question.

"I did what was best for my son at the time."

Jacob crossed his eyebrows. "This is all too much. I am really disappointed in you and mum," he said.

The older lady looked at Olivia.

"This is your fault. My Jacob would have never spoken to me like that. Why did you have to come here?" she said to her.

"My mother felt it was right for me to know that I had a father."

"How do I even know that you really are his daughter?"

"We can get a DNA test done."

"You are rude." She shook her head. Olivia did not think that she had been rude to her.

"I apologize if I sound rude," said Olivia.

"You should just go back to America. There is no place for you here," said their grandmother.

"Nana, that is rude," Jacob chided. Olivia was not even bothered at this point. Far too many people had said that to her.

"I knew that my actions would haunt me one day," said their grandmother. She gently touched her face. Olivia saw the almond-shaped birth mark on her grandmother's wrist, just like the one she had on hers. Sheikh Solomon had told her about it before.

"What did you not like about my mother? The fact that she was from a poor background or because she was American and not Arabic?" Olivia asked. Jacob's eyes widened. He just leaned back in his seat.

"Do you think I am a racist?" their grandmother asked.

"Possibly," said Olivia. Jacob's eyes widened and he just looked at the floor. "If your son was happy with Elizabeth, then why would you tear them apart? Because of you I grew up without a father," she said.

"It was not my intention for you to grow up fatherless. I was only thinking about my son and my family's reputation."

Olivia tried her hardest not to roll her eyes. She was sick and tired of these rich people telling her about reputation. They thought so highly of themselves. Everyone was equal. No one was more important than the other.

"You people only think about yourselves," said Olivia.

"Did you come here for recognition?" her grandmother asked.

"No, I came here to let you know that I have become reacquainted with my father." That was the first time she had referred to Sheikh Solomon as her father. "Your plan to keep me away from him failed," she said as she rose to her feet.

"You are just as fiery as your mother."

"I am my mother's daughter. Excuse me." Olivia walked out of the room and into the corridor. She headed towards the front door and let herself out. Jacob's driver opened the door for Olivia. She climbed in and sat in the backseat.

Olivia did not even know what to feel. Her so-called grandmother was not even apologetic about her actions. Instead of apologizing or something along those lines, she defended her actions. Once again

Olivia found herself wanting to see Joseph. He was the first person that she had thought of talking to about this entire messy situation.

Jacob opened the car door and joined her in the car. "Well, that was awkward," he said as he shut the door. Olivia laughed a little.

"Maybe we should not have come," she said.

"No, it's good we came."

The driver started the engine and drove off.

"It's annoying to have to keep going through this conversation again and again," said Olivia. She was tired of having to talk about being the illegitimate daughter of Sheikh Solomon. She hoped that it was the last time she had to explain herself and have some nasty remarks thrown in her face.

"I understand you," Jacob replied. "I feel weird about my mother seducing my father. If she never got pregnant with me, then they would not be together."

"I can't imagine how that feels." It was true. She couldn't imagine it and she did not want to.

"I never noticed much love between my parents. Now I understand why."

Olivia placed her hand on his. She felt bad that he grew up in a loveless home. No child deserved that.

Elizabeth was the only woman Sheikh Solomon had ever loved. Olivia felt bad that her presence had brought all those secrets to light.

"I'm sorry," she said quietly.

"It's not your fault." Jacob sighed. "What happens in the dark will always come to light," he added. Olivia nodded. She very much agreed with that statement.

Jacob and Olivia arrived back home just after 9 p.m. They both headed into the house and went to their bedrooms. Olivia felt tired and drained. It had been a very eventful day and she just wanted to lie down.

It was about half past nine when the maid came with the house phone and told her that Joseph was on the phone.

"Why are you calling me this late?" she asked Joseph. She was screaming with joy on the inside. She was so happy that he had called her. She had been wanting to speak to him.

"It is very odd having to call you on the house phone all the time," he said. Olivia laughed a little.

"Yes it is," she agreed. She was used to speaking to people on her cell phone.

"How did you find lunch with my father?"

"It was fine."

"Really?" Joseph sounded shocked.

"No, he's a scary man," Olivia confessed. Joseph laughed a little.

"Yes he is, but from what I heard, you handled yourself well."

"What did he say?" Olivia was quite curious to know what Joseph's father thought of her.

"He thinks that you're an intelligent woman with impressive valor," he said. Olivia burst into laughter.

"Valor? I guess he expected me to shake in his presence."

"Most people do."

"That does not surprise me."

"Why did you not tell him that you did not want to marry me?" Joseph asked.

"That's for you to tell him," she replied.

"Maybe I won't have to tell him."

Olivia started laughing. She knew what he was going to say next. "Joseph, I will admit that I do like you but I don't know if I'm ready to marry you." The words just came out of her mouth so easily. She never wanted to tell a man that she liked him first. However, she did not want to send mixed signals. She always wanted to be clear.

"That's the nicest thing you have ever said to me," Joseph replied. Olivia started laughing. She knew well that she had never showered him with compliments.

"Is it really?" she asked sarcastically.

"Yes," he replied. "Now that you told me you like me, I am pleased. That means we feel the same way about each other."

"Do you like me?" Olivia asked boldly. She did not want to assume anything. She wanted to hear the words straight from him.

"Yes, Olivia, I like you very much," he said; his voice was so low and sexy as always. She felt butterflies in her stomach. His words made her happy.

"Okay," she said casually; trying to mask how happy she was in that moment.

"I have to go to Egypt tomorrow for business and to see Jasmine. I will be there for a few days."

"That'll be nice." A small part of Olivia was not happy with the idea of Joseph going away on business. She wanted to see him the next day. Now she was having to wait for a few days.

"Come with me," said Joseph.

"What? Why?"

"I want you with me."

"I guess it'll be nice to get away for a while." She felt happy that he had asked her. That way, they would spend some time together.

"Good, I'll get a car for you in the morning."

Chapter 23

Joseph was leaning against his car as he waited for Olivia and Amir. His jet was getting fueled up before they took off for Egypt. His phone vibrated in his pocket. He slid his hand into his pocket and fished it out. It was a message from Ruth, a woman he once had a relationship with. The message said that she wanted to see him. Joseph just erased the message and slipped his phone back in his pocket. He was used to women always vying for his attention.

Amir arrived before Olivia. He got out of the car and approached Joseph. "Hey," he said as he stood next to him.

"You're here," said Joseph.

"Your lady isn't here yet? I'm shocked that she agreed to come."

"She's been very cooperative recently," Joseph said with a smile.

"She's falling for you," said Amir.

"She met with my father yesterday."

"How did that go?"

"He said that she boldly speaks her mind and there is something about her that he likes."

"Really? That is shocking."

Joseph agreed. He too was shocked that their meeting had gone the way it did. "Yeah, but he doesn't like the fact that she is an illegitimate child," he added.

"That can't be helped," said Amir.

Olivia arrived just then. She jumped out of the car and quickly walked towards Joseph. She had on leggings and a hoody. Nothing she wore shocked him anymore. She approached him and stood in front of him and Amir.

"Good morning," she said to Amir. "It's been a while since we've met."

"It has." Amir leaned forward and kissed her on both cheeks. "I hope you've been well."

"I have been." Olivia smiled.

"Shouldn't you greet me first?" Joseph asked her. He wanted to be the first person she saw and talked to. Olivia smiled guiltily.

"I haven't seen him for a while. It is politer for me to greet him first." She touched his arm. "How are you?" she asked.

"I'm fine," he said. He leaned closer to Olivia and kissed her on the forehead.

After the private jet had been fueled up, they all boarded. Joseph and Olivia sat next to each other, and Amir sat opposite them. The journey only took an hour and a few minutes. There were two cars already waiting for them when they arrived. Olivia left in one car and headed to the hotel they were staying at. Amir and Joseph left in the other car and headed to their meeting. They were meeting with an Egyptian oil company to renew their contracts.

***

Later that day after their meeting, Joseph, Amir and Olivia went to visit Jasmine. She was volunteering at an orphanage just outside the capital city. The drive took them about two hours.

"Feels good to be out of the car," Olivia said as she stretched. She had changed into a pair of shorts and a white T-shirt and white sneakers. Her hair was tied up into two ponytails.

"The journey was not that long," Joseph said to her.

"Two hours is a long time."

"Are you one of those people that cannot stay still for long periods of time?" Amir asked her.

"Yes." Olivia laughed.

Joseph looked around. The orphanage was not an extravagant place. It rather looked like an abandoned place that had been long forgotten. The paint on the buildings had chipped off. There were no lawns, just dusty land.

Jasmine walked out of the building. When she saw them, she immediately ran towards them. "Hi guys," she said.

"What kind of place is this?" Joseph asked.

"An orphanage, Joseph."

"Even if it is an orphanage, it does not have to look so derelict," said Amir. Olivia and Jasmine looked at each other in shock.

"An orphanage is not a five-star hotel," Olivia pointed out.

"They are just used to seeing nice things. Welcome to reality," said Jasmine. She opened her arms and walked towards Olivia. She wrapped her arms around her. "I am glad you came as well," she said.

"How have you been?" Olivia asked as Jasmine released her from her embrace.

"I've been good," Jasmine smiled. "You are just in time for lunch," she said.

"You want us to have lunch here?" Joseph asked.

"Why not?"

"I can think of many reasons," said Amir.

Olivia shook her head. "I am actually hungry. I would not mind eating now," she said.

"Good, let's go." Jasmine took Olivia's hand in hers and led the way. Joseph and Amir looked at each other before they followed.

The dining room was of modest size. The children were sitting at the long wooden tables. They were eating pita bread, chickpeas and lamb. They did not have much food on their plates. Joseph felt bad because he always ate so well.

"Today is lamb day," said Jasmine. "They have it once a month."

"Just once a month?" Olivia asked.

"Yes. Let's get our trays." Jasmine confidently picked up a tray and a plate and joined the line. Olivia followed. Joseph and Amir hesitated.

"I never thought I would be lining up in a canteen for food," Joseph said to Amir.

"Neither did I," Amir replied. The two of them picked up the grey trays and joined the line. Joseph felt weird as the canteen ladies dished food out for him. They stared at him oddly. They were probably wondering why he was there too.

After he got his food, Joseph followed Olivia and Jasmine to the table. There were children sitting at the table also. It was awkward for Joseph. He had never had to share a table with strangers. On this occasion, it was him that was intruding. Amir came with his tray and sat down next to Joseph.

"What do you do here?" Olivia asked Jasmine.

"I teach English," she replied.

"What made you want to do this?"

"I come from a wealthy family. I grew up with everything," said Jasmine. "My heart broke when I saw how other people live. So I try to give back."

Olivia smiled and nodded. "That is amazing. We need more people like you in the world," she said. As Jasmine and Olivia talked, Joseph realized that they were quite alike.

"How does the food taste?" Jasmine asked.

"Odd," Joseph replied.

"The pita bread is pretty good," Olivia replied. She was almost finished eating.

"You can eat anything," Joseph said.

Olivia burst into laughter. "It is because you are used to eating the finest of foods but I am not. You're such a snob," she said. In that moment, Joseph decided that he was going to donate money to that orphanage. It was because he knew Olivia did not have it easy growing up. Joseph wanted to be a better man for her. He wanted to be the man that understood where she came from and what she went through. He had learned that she was not impressed by money and flashy things. All she wanted was a good heart.

After they were finished eating, Jasmine and Olivia went to play basketball with the teenaged children outside. Joseph was pleasantly surprised to see that Olivia was good at basketball. Somehow, he had thought that she was not good at sports. She looked so pretty as she ran with the ball. Joseph found himself smiling.

Joseph walked off and went to the car. He retrieved his leather briefcase and searched for his checkbook. He took it with him and went to find the reception area.

"Excuse me, if I want to make a donation, to whom do I make the check out?" he asked the lady sitting behind the wooden desk that looked like it was going fall at any moment.

"To St. Mary's Orphanage," she said as she sprang up to her feet. Joseph quickly filled out the check. He tore it out of the book and handed it to the woman. She looked at it and gasped.

"Take care," Joseph said as he turned on his heel to leave.

"Sir!" She called out. "Are you sure you want to donate this much?" she asked. He had made the check out for five hundred thousand dollars.

"Yes," he replied plainly.

"Thank you so much. May God bless you," she replied. "Truly, sir, thank you. We have never received this much money. Thank you."

Joseph smiled and walked off. He wasn't looking for recognition or praise. He simply wanted to donate.

Chapter 24

Joseph and Olivia went for a stroll in Alexandria before they left Egypt. The days had flown by, she did not want to leave. It felt so nice to just be there with him. It was nice to be without the drama from Daaliyah and her daughters.

"Are you hungry?" Joseph asked Olivia.

"Why would you ask me that?" she asked him.

"You are always hungry."

Olivia laughed a little. It was quite true. She was always hungry. "Not right now," she replied. She was still full from the brunch they had had with Amir.

"I guess you will be hungry soon," said Joseph. Olivia smiled and slid her hand in the pocket of her shorts. Alexandria was beautiful, she thought to herself. They were walking along the pavement next to the Red Sea. The waters were a nice blue color. The wind was blowing through Olivia's hair. It was a such refreshing feeling.

"I would love to come back here," she said. She wanted to come back and explore the place.

"If you want we can stay longer," said Joseph.

"No, you have to return to work."

"We can come back anytime you want."

Olivia smiled. She did not mind coming back with Joseph. It was amazing being with him. She was able to forget all that was wrong with her life.

"I handed in my resignation, well more like e-mailed it," she said to him. Joseph stopped walking and faced Olivia. He gently tugged on her arm to stop her from walking. She stopped and looked at him.

"When?" he asked her.

"On Monday," she replied. She had sent the e-mail the same day they had left for Egypt. It was now Friday and she thought it was time to tell Joseph.

"And you are just telling me now?" he asked in disbelief.

Olivia burst into laughter.

"Sorry, it just wasn't important at the time," she said.

"So you will stay here?" He snaked his arm around her waist and pulled her closer to him. Olivia nodded as she wrapped her arms around his neck. She definitely wanted to stay in Lebanon longer, with him. Joseph smiled. He was so handsome, he made her shy every time he smiled at her.

"Jasmine told me that you donated money to the orphanage," she said to him.

"Oh, did she?" he asked. Olivia was positively impressed and surprised when she had found out that he had donated the money without telling her or Jasmine or even Amir. He had just done it, which showed her that his intentions were pure. He hadn't done it for praise. Jasmine had found out when she helped with the administrative work. She had seen the check.

"She did. That was such an amazing thing you did," said Olivia.

"I guess."

"It influenced my decision to stay. I want to be with a man that is kind-hearted."

"I am happy that you came to this decision." His green eyes searched her hazel eyes. He dipped his head lower and gently touched her lips with his. Olivia closed her eyes and let him kiss her. He kissed her so softly and passionately. His lips were soft. Olivia's knees buckled with pleasure. She rested her body against his to stop from falling over.

Olivia broke off the kiss. "It was not an easy one to make," she said to him.

"I know; you are very stubborn," he said to her.

They kept walking, this time holding hands. Olivia felt so girly and just wanted to giggle. She had never been the girl to get a man like Joseph. He was handsome, tall, muscular and rich. He was the complete opposite of the type of men she normally attracted. She just wanted to scream at the top of her lungs that he was her man, HERS.

***

Joseph's car parked right outside Sheikh Solomon's house later that day. Olivia looked outside and sighed. It was time for her to return to the house. "I have to go," she said reluctantly.

"You sound sad to be leaving me," Joseph said with a smirk on his face.

Olivia smiled and rolled her eyes at him.

"It's not always about you," she said.

"It should be." Joseph took Olivia's hand into his and kissed it. Olivia smiled.

"I think you are sadder to let me go," she said playfully.

"Of course I am." Joseph caressed Olivia's face with the back of his hand. He leaned closer to her and kissed her forehead. "I can't wait to make you my wife and have you live with me," he added. The thought of being his wife made her smile.

"Be patient," she said. Joseph pressed his face against hers. Olivia closed her eyes and breathed in his manly scent.

"It's hard. I want you. I want every bit of you." He kissed her lips. Olivia placed her hands on his face. Even the stubble of his beard felt good in her hands.

"Your face feels nice." Olivia giggled and pressed a kiss against his cheek. Joseph pulled Olivia closer to him and kissed her lips. It always felt so good when Joseph kissed her. He smelled so nice and his lips were just amazing. He was amazing.

Finally, Olivia and Joseph stopped kissing. "I'll see you soon," she said and opened the door.

"Okay, habibi," he said. Olivia smiled as she got out of the car. She had learned that habibi meant darling. It was the first time Joseph had called her that and it made her heart melt.

***

Olivia's bubble of happiness burst when she walked into the house. Everyone was in the drawing room, including Sheikh Solomon's mother. Olivia attempted to walk past the drawing room but Daaliyah called her in.

"Why did you think it was a good idea to just go and see nana Solomon?" she asked Olivia.

"It was my idea," said Jacob.

"Why would you encourage such a thing?"

"What is wrong with them going to see their grandmother?" Sheikh Solomon asked. He genuinely looked confused.

"It's the disrespect that I received," said grandma Solomon. Jacob and Olivia looked at each other in disbelief.

"Disrespect?" Jacob asked.

"Yes, I felt disrespected in my own home."

"What exactly happened?" Sheikh Solomon asked. Olivia just stood in the doorway of the drawing room.

"Olivia and I found out that mother and nana were the ones who chased Elizabeth back to America when they found out that she was with child," said Jacob. Sheikh Solomon's face went pale. He stood there in shock. Olivia felt bad for him. No one wanted to hear that their mother had betrayed them.

"That is not true!" Daaliyah protested. Her face turned red. She looked at her husband and shook her head.

"We did what we felt was necessary," said grandma Solomon. Olivia shook her head. The old woman was unapologetic.

"Mother!" Daaliyah breathed.

"Jacob, what did you just say?" Sheikh Solomon asked his son.

"Olivia and I overheard mother speaking to Esther about it," said Jacob. Rania and Marina were just staring at their mother in shock.

"I did what was necessary to keep my family's dignity," said grandma Solomon. "She was a nice girl but she was not right for you."

"Right for me? As a result of your actions, my daughter grew up without a father," said Sheikh Solomon.

"You've been married to Daaliyah for all these years. There is no use regretting it now."

"You could have at least told me that I had a daughter out there." Sheikh Solomon looked so disappointed and upset. He turned on his heel and left the room. Olivia felt very awkward, and she did not know what to do. She felt bad for the sheikh. He had been separated from the woman he loved. Olivia also felt bad for Jacob. It must be hard to know that your mother was second best, that she had to get rid of another woman in order to secure her position as your father's wife.

Olivia left the room also. She just did not want to be part of any more drama.

Chapter 25

Joseph sighed as he walked into his parents' house on the following Sunday afternoon. Sunday lunches were starting to be awkward for him to attend. He did not want to get into a dispute over his marriage. He was not going to change his mind and his mother needed to accept that.

"Good afternoon, sheikh," one of the maids greeted him as he walked through the front door.

"Hello," he replied. He headed towards the dining room. His parents were already seated at the table.

"Hello Joseph," his father greeted him.

"Good afternoon, Father," said Joseph. He approached his mother and kissed her on the cheek. "I trust that you have been well." he said to her as he sat down.

"I haven't been well," she replied. Joseph wanted to tell her to stop being petty but he could not do that. Instead he just looked at her and touched her hand.

"Why haven't you been well? What is the matter?" he asked, even though he knew that it was because of Olivia.

"I am not happy about your poor choice in women," she replied.

"Father met her, and he liked her. Why don't you do the same?" Joseph had to bring his father into the conversation. He needed his father to be on his side. Esther looked at her husband.

"You did not tell me that you liked her," she said to him.

"I never said that I liked her," Joseph's father replied.

"I thought you approved of her," said Joseph as he started eating. His father crossed his eyebrows.

"You approve?" Esther was really not happy.

"I said she is an intelligent girl," said Joseph's father.

"She is an opportunistic jezebel!"

"I do not think she is interested in his wealth."

"Everyone is."

"I got a different vibe from her." The older sheikh sighed. "Although she is not full Arabic and is an illegitimate child, she has integrity and intelligence," he added.

"And?"

"And Joseph is not willing to let her go. So we might as well approve of the marriage."

Esther dropped her fork onto her plate. "Over my dead body!" she spat out.

"Esther, don't be so dramatic. It will not be the end of the world," said her husband. Joseph just ate and let them argue with each other.

"How am I being dramatic? You want my son to marry that woman?"

"He wants to marry her. We don't have to like it but at least he is finally growing up."

"No, I do not like it," said Esther.

"At least give Olivia a chance. You know nothing of her and yet you loathe her with passion," said Joseph.

"I have heard enough from Daaliyah," said Esther.

"Did you not hear that Daaliyah was the one who seduced Sheikh Solomon just so he would leave Olivia's mother?"

"Watch your mouth! You cannot be saying things like that about Daaliyah," said Joseph's father. Esther barely reacted.

"But it's the truth and mother knows it."

Joseph's father looked at his wife. "It's true?" he asked when he saw her reaction. He surprised Joseph when he started laughing.

"Why is that funny?" Joseph asked.

"This entire situation is very twisted," he said. He laughed even harder. Esther looked at her son.

"He's gone mad," she said to him.

"I am sick of all of this. Olivia and Joseph will wed next month. That is my final say on the matter."

Joseph almost leaped out of his chair in excitement. Whenever his father said it was his final say on the matter, it really was. No one dared to challenge him. They just nodded and did as told.

"Fine, but you will regret this," said Esther.

"Thank you, Father; you will not regret this," said Joseph.

"I better not," his father replied.

For a few minutes, there was silence and peace. They all ate their food quietly. Joseph was just on cloud nine. He was so happy about being able to marry Olivia; soon. He wanted her out of that house, away from Daaliyah and her evil daughters.

The past week had been good for Joseph. He had enjoyed being able to see Olivia every day and spending time with her. She was fun to be around, she made him forget all the stress of work. She put him in a better mood. She was kind-hearted. When they had gone to the orphanage, he had learned that she was good at basketball and she was good with the children.

One of the maids walked into the room and announced that there was a visitor that wanted an audience with Joseph urgently. "Are you allowing just anyone here these days?" Joseph asked.

"It's someone from your past. She has been before, so we thought it was okay to let her in," said the maid.

"Her?"

"Hudah," said the maid. Joseph stopped eating. He wiped his mouth with his napkin and rose to his feet at once.

Hudah was a woman he once had a relationship with. That was the longest relationship he ever had. She wanted marriage and he did not. And so they broke up. He wondered why she was back in his life.

"I remember Hudah," said Esther. "Why is she here?"

"I don't know but I must find out," Joseph replied. He quickly headed to the drawing room.

Hudah was standing in the drawing room. She was tall and slim but curvy. She was still as beautiful as before. She had long, silky dark hair. She had an amazing olive skin tone. She always looked after herself. She made sure to keep her body in shape and always looked after her skin.

"Hudah," Joseph said as he approached her.

"Joseph," she breathed. "I needed to see you." She reached out to touch Joseph's face but he moved away.

"How did you even know that I was here?" he asked.

"I remember that you have your family Sunday lunches here," she said with a smile.

"Why did you need to see me?" he asked. Why was it urgent? Joseph was curious. Hudah took a deep breath and straightened out her coral-colored dress.

"There is no easy way to say this," she said.

"Then just say it."

"I have a son."

"Okay?" Joseph wondered why that had anything to do with him. He slid his hands in his pockets and waited for her to elaborate.

"He is two and a half years old."

"Congratulations," Joseph said sarcastically.

"He is yours."

"Excuse me?"

"Luke; he is your son," she said.

Joseph crossed his eyebrows. Maybe he was not hearing her correctly.

"My son?" he asked.

"Yes. He is your son."

"Then why would you only tell me now?"

"I couldn't bring myself to tell you before. You did not want marriage and I did," she said.

Joseph frowned at her.

"That is not even a plausible excuse," he said to her.

Hudah shrugged her shoulders. "Well, Luke is your son," she said. "There is nothing either one of us can do about it."

"Joseph, what did she just say?" Esther asked her son as she walked into the room. Joseph cussed under his breath. He had just ended the drama about Olivia with his mother, and now there was Hudah. His mother was not going to swallow that pill easily.

"Hello, Mrs. Boutros," said Hudah. "Joseph and I have a son."

Esther's eyes widened. She looked at Joseph and then back at Hudah.

"That is not possible," she said.

"It is very possible, it happened."

"I don't believe you."

"Maybe I should I have come with him," said Hudah.

"That would have made sense," said Joseph.

Hudah pulled out her phone and swiped it to unlock the screen. She showed it to Joseph. There was a picture of a little boy. "That proves nothing to me," he said.

"I need to sit down," said Esther. She stumbled over to the sofa and plunked herself down.

"I did not mean to surprise you like this," said Hudah.

"And yet you did."

"I kept him away for selfish reasons and it wasn't right. A child should not grow up without their father, and so here I am."

"How do we even know that it really is his child?" Esther asked.

"I am happy to have him take a DNA test."

Joseph closed his eyes and tilted his head back. How was he going to tell Olivia?

Chapter 26

Joseph felt anxious as he stared at the little boy before him. A thousand thoughts raced through his mind. Was that little boy his? What would life be like if that boy was actually his? It worried him what Olivia's reaction was going to be like. What if she left him?

Joseph had demanded a DNA test. He wasn't just going to be in that boy's life without solid proof that he was the father. So the next morning Joseph and Hudah along with her son had gone to Joseph's doctor for a DNA test. It had to be Joseph's doctor. It had to be under his terms.

"Please come in," said Dr. Amari. They walked into her office and sat at her desk.

"Thank you for seeing us at such short notice," Joseph said to her. He trusted her because she had been his doctor since birth, and she had signed a non-disclosure agreement. She could not sell his stories to the press or anything like that.

"It is no problem, Sheikh Boutros," she replied. She put on gloves and opened a plastic packet. She pulled out a swab and swabbed the little boy's mouth, then put the swab in a clear plastic bag. She did the same for Joseph. Then she also took blood samples.

"When can we expect the results?" Joseph asked her.

"I can have them later today," she replied. Joseph nodded. The sooner, the better. He did not like waiting around for things. He looked at the little boy sitting on Hudah's lap.

"Say hi," Hudah said to her son.

"Hi," her son said to Joseph. He felt so many mixed emotions. He could not even respond. He just rose to his feet and left the room.

Joseph got in his car and went to Sheikh Solomon's house. Olivia was the only person he wanted to see at that moment. As he arrived, he ran into Rania at the front door. She must have been on her way out because she was all dressed up in expensive clothes and a lot of makeup.

"Sheikh Boutros," she breathed.

"Hi Rania," he said. She approached him and wrapped her arms around his neck and pressed her body against him. Joseph felt a shiver running down his spine.

"What are you doing?" he asked her.

"Isn't it obvious? I am hugging you."

"Why?"

"I want you to feel the embrace of a true woman."

Joseph gently pushed her away from him. He was in no mood for games. "Please, don't do that ever again," he said to her. He wanted to be as polite as he could be.

"Why would you want to marry Olivia?" she spat out. "She is a nobody!"

"That is no polite way to speak of your older sister."

"She is not my sister! She is nothing but an illegitimate child. She came into our lives and destroyed everything. Now she has taken what is mine."

"What of yours did she take?"

"You."

Joseph raised his eyebrows. He was never hers. He was never going to marry her. It was crazy but not surprising to learn that she thought of him as hers.

"I am not yours," he said quietly.

"Please, Joseph." She took his hand and put it on her breast. "Come to me."

Joseph immediately yanked his hand back.

"I do not appreciate you talking negatively about Olivia, nor do I appreciate you acting like you work in a brothel," he said. He was already annoyed about Hudah's sudden appearance and now Rania was making it worse. He walked into the house but then he stopped. "One more thing, never call me by my first name," he said to her and then walked off.

"Hello, Sheikh Boutros," a blushing maid greeted him as he walked in.

"Hi, where is Olivia?" he asked.

"She is in her room. Shall I call her down for you?"

"No, take me to her room."

"Yes sir."

Joseph followed the maid upstairs. He had been to Sheikh Solomon's house many times but he had never been upstairs. The maid looked back at him and smiled. Then she looked forward. Joseph shook his head. Even though she knew that he was betrothed to Olivia, she was still trying to get his attention.

They finally came to a halt in front of a white door with a golden knob. The maid knocked on the door. "I'll take it from here," he said to her. She nodded before she walked off.

"Come in!" Olivia shouted. Joseph turned the golden knob and then walked in. Olivia was sitting in tiny shorts and a T-shirt on her bed. She turned her head and gasped when she saw him. "Joseph!" she breathed.

"Hi," he said softly. Olivia put her laptop on her nightstand and sat up. Joseph sat on the bed next to her.

"This is a surprise," she said with a smile.

"I wanted to see you."

Olivia took his face into her hands and searched his eyes. "What is the matter?" she asked.

"Nothing," he replied.

"No, there is something definitely going on with you," she said. Joseph raised an eyebrow. She was able to tell there was something wrong. No one else could because he was so good at putting on a poker face.

"A woman from my past," he said.

"Okay, what about her?"

"If I tell you, promise me that you will not leave me."

Olivia jerked her head backwards a little. "Surely, it is not that bad," she said.

"I don't know how you will take it." He sighed.

Olivia leaned forward and pressed a small kiss against his lips. "You can tell me anything," she said to him.

"I was in a relationship with a woman named Hudah a few years ago."

"Okay, go on."

"I just found out that she has a son and I might be the father."

Olivia raised her eyebrows. "Whoa," she said. She looked so shocked. There was silence for a moment. Joseph felt nervous. He wondered what she was thinking. "You might be or you are definitely the father?" she asked him.

"Might. We went for a DNA test today," he said to her. She nodded quietly. "I'm sorry," he added. Those were the only words that came to mind. He did not know what to say or do.

Olivia leaned towards him and wrapped her arms around his neck. "Don't apologize to me," she said gently. "This is something that happened before we knew each other."

Joseph looked at her and searched her eyes. He had not expected such a warm reaction from her. "I did not expect you to react this way," he said.

She smiled.

"You thought I'd get mad?" she asked.

"Honestly, I did not know what to expect."

She kissed his forehead and then his cheek. "Don't ever feel like you can't tell me anything. No matter what it is, you must tell me," she said.

He cleared his throat. "There is one more thing," he said.

Olivia released him from her embrace. "What?" she asked. He told her about Rania. Olivia frowned. "Remind me to slap her later," she said.

Joseph chuckled a little. "You want to slap her?" he asked.

"Of course! How dare she?"

Joseph smiled and pressed a small kiss against her lips. She was so adorable. Olivia pulled him closer and kissed him. He wrapped his arms around her and held her tightly as they kissed. He felt so sane and relaxed in her arms. Only she could lighten his mood so easily.

***

"The DNA test showed a 97% match," Joseph said to his parents the following day at the breakfast table. His parents both stopped eating and looked at him.

"Joseph, how many more surprises are you going to throw at us?" Esther asked him.

"I did not plan this. It is a surprise to me also," he replied.

"You should have been careful," his father said to him.

"I know; I regret not taking extra precautions." Joseph was not pleased about the entire situation. Just when things were going great with Olivia, Hudah had to come along. It angered him that he had not been careful when he was with her. He was also angry that she had not told him about it until now.

"What is the point regretting it now?" his mother asked him. "You have no other choice but to right your wrongs."

"What do you mean by that?"

"You must marry her of course."

"What?" Joseph spat out. He whipped his head in his father's direction. "Father!" he said.

"I am sorry, son, but I am with your mother on this one," his father replied.

Joseph dropped his fork onto his plate.

"I can't marry Hudah. I will not marry her!"

"So you want your son, my grandson, to grow up as an illegitimate child. I will not allow that to happen," said his father.

Joseph was trying to stay calm but it was not working. His hands started shaking with anger.

"I cannot lose Olivia all because the two of you care about your reputation more than my happiness," he said as he rose from the table.

"You will not speak to me like that," said his father. Joseph had never been disrespectful to his father but he was furious. "I will not force you into anything. It's your choice," he added.

"Habibi, what are you saying?" Esther said to her husband.

"Thank you," said Joseph.

"Let me finish." Joseph's father paused for a moment. "If you marry Hudah, you will inherit my oil company. If you marry Olivia, you will inherit nothing."

Esther gasped loudly and placed her hand over her mouth. She looked like she was going to pass out in shock.

Joseph raised his eyebrows. After everything he had done for the company, he wondered how his father could give him such an ultimatum. "Expect my resignation on your desk later today," he said.

"Joseph!" his mother screamed. Joseph stormed out of the room. The company wasn't worth it if he had to give up the only person he had ever fallen in love with.

Chapter 27

Olivia was at Joseph's house cooking for him. Even though he had a chef and maids, she liked cooking for him and doing small things for him like that. She especially now wanted to do things for him because she knew that he was going through a hard time with Hudah. Finding out that he had a son was not easy. She had seen her father go through it when he found out about her.

"What are you doing here?" a voice sounded from behind Olivia. She recognized the icy voice immediately. She turned around.

"Good afternoon, Mrs. Boutros," said Olivia. She forced herself to smile.

"I said what are you doing here?"

"I came to cook for Joseph."

"He has a chef."

"I like cooking for him, and he likes me cooking for him," she said. Mrs. Boutros slightly frowned.

"Where is my son?" she asked.

"He is at work."

"No, he is not. I was just there."

"Maybe he is at a meeting," said Olivia. She wondered why his mother was looking for him in the middle of the day.

"I doubt that," his mother spat out. "He handed in his resignation."

Olivia almost burst into laughter. "How can he hand in a resignation to his own father?" It made no sense to her. Joseph loved his job. Why would he quit?

"It's all because of you," said Esther.

"Me?"

"I am sure you know about Luke, his son."

"Yes."

"Joseph's father and I do not want our grandson to grow up without his father," she said.

Olivia understood what she was saying. However, she wondered what it had to do with her. Why would that make Joseph quit his job?

"Of course. I understand what it's like," said Olivia.

"I want him to marry Hudah."

That's when it hit her. Joseph's mother wanted Joseph to marry Hudah but Joseph had refused. That was why Joseph's mother was blaming her.

"How does he feel about that?" Olivia asked.

"He refused."

"But why did he quit?"

"Because his father gave him an ultimatum. He was to either marry Hudah and inherit the company or marry you and inherit nothing."

Olivia gasped. She placed her hand on her heart. That was something too big to give up. She most certainly did not want him to give up his rightful place because of her.

"Joseph," she whispered. She felt so bad for him.

"You have ruined my son's life. Please stop now and just go back to America," said Mrs. Boutros.

"The only thing I did was fall in love with your son," Olivia said honestly. Mrs. Boutros was being too unfair to her. She had not ruined his life. She had not forced him into anything.

"Love?" said Mrs. Boutros.

"Yes, I love Joseph so much. I would never want him to give up anything for me."

Mrs. Boutros stared at the teary-eyed Olivia for a moment. She held her by her shoulders. "I may have misjudged you," she said.

"I did not fit the part you wanted your daughter-in-law to play," she said.

"No, you did not." Mrs. Boutros sighed. She slowly got down on her knees. Olivia's eyes flew open.

"What are you doing?" she asked her.

"Joseph is my only child. Only he can inherit the company, and his son needs a father. Please go back to Atlanta. This is the only way he can give up on you," she said. Olivia felt incredibly uncomfortable seeing Joseph's mother on her knees begging her to leave her son. She thought Joseph's mother was being a bit too dramatic but Joseph had worked hard to inherit that company. She understood that his mother would not want him to throw all of that away.

"I love him so much; I don't want to leave him," said Olivia. A tear rolled down from her eye. History was repeating itself. Twenty-three years ago, her mother was faced with a similar decision. When she found out that Sheikh Solomon's mother had asked her mother to leave, she thought that if she was ever in that situation she would not leave. She thought she would stay and fight for the man she loved. However, now that it was happening to her, she completely understood her mother's decisions.

"I don't want him to lose his rightful position," said Olivia. She closed her eyes as the tears streamed down her face.

"I'm sorry. I have to do what is best for my son."

It was funny how many times Olivia had heard that. However, everyone that was saying it, was only doing what was best for themselves. Olivia wiped the tears from her face.

"Goodbye, Mrs. Boutros," she said. It was not a pleasure to meet her. Olivia quickly walked off.

She returned to Sheikh Solomon's house and packed her things. It was best for her to leave as soon as possible. If she saw Joseph once more, she was not going to be able to leave.

Jacob drove her to the airport. He had failed to convince Olivia to stay. However, she agreed to stay in touch with him and Sheikh Solomon.

"It's nice having an older sister," Jacob said to Olivia before she got on the plane. Olivia smiled. She was happy that Jacob considered her his older sister unlike Rania and Marina. They treated Olivia horribly.

"It's nice to have a sibling. It was not always fun being an only child," she replied.

"Take care of yourself." Jacob pulled Olivia into his arms and rubbed her head.

"I will," she said with a smile. A tear rolled down her cheek. She pulled out of his embrace and wiped the tear from her cheek. She waved at him and went to board her flight.

The flight to Atlanta was very long and sad for Olivia. All she could think about was Joseph. She remembered the first time she had seen him and how she had felt. She had never fallen so fast and hard for any man before. She knew that she was never going to experience love like that ever again. Love like that came once in a lifetime.

When Olivia arrived at her apartment in Atlanta, she immediately called Daya over.

***

Olivia lay on the sofa; numb from the pain of leaving Joseph. It was the hardest thing she had ever had to do. She tried telling herself that Joseph probably did not feel about her the way she felt about him. However, it was not working. She could not stop crying.

"Have something to eat," Daya said to her as she walked into the living room with a plate of food. As soon as Olivia had called, Daya rushed over and spent the night trying to comfort Olivia but it was not working.

"I should have left the first time I said I would leave," said Olivia. Daya sat on the sofa next to her and rubbed her back.

"Don't try and blame yourself. All of them are evil."

"The same thing that had happened to my mother is happening to me. I understand her now. I see why she left and never looked back."

"I can't believe that Joseph was willing to give it all up for you. He really loved you."

Suddenly there was a loud knock on the door. Olivia almost jumped out of her skin. "Tell them to go away," she said to Daya.

"Could it be the postman or something?" Daya mumbled as she rose to her feet. Olivia heard Daya open the door and then gasp really loudly. "Joseph!" she breathed. Olivia sat up immediately. She saw Joseph walking into the room.

"Joseph? What are you doing here?" she asked.

"Same thing I want to ask you," he replied as he approached her. He kneeled down on one knee and took her hands into his. "How could you leave me like that?" he asked.

"I had to." Olivia started crying. "I couldn't let you just give up on your company like that."

"That means nothing to me without you." Joseph searched Olivia's eyes.

"It was all too much. I thought I could handle it, but I could not. It was hard living with Daaliyah and her daughters. It was hard knowing that your mother hated me, and now she wanted you to marry Hudah. It was all too much for me."

"I get it," said Joseph. "I hadn't been fair. I said I would protect you but I failed."

"It's not your fault. You did the best you could do."

Joseph shook his head. "I don't want to marry Hudah. I don't want to inherit the company at the price of losing you. I don't want to lose you, I can't, Olivia. I need you."

Olivia could see sincerity in Joseph's eyes. She needed him too.

"Joseph," she whispered. She held his face in the palm of her hands.

"I love you, Olivia Grant. You have taught me what it means to love someone and to be loved. If my parents can't accept that, then I don't care. I can settle down in Atlanta and start my life here, with you."

"What will you do?" she asked him.

"I don't know but at least I will be with you."

"Joseph, you cannot just up and leave your life. You cannot give up on everything just for me. I will not allow you to do that," she yelled.

"I can and I have. I love you, damnit, and no one will stop me from marrying you. I am not going back home just to marry a woman I do not love. I am not going anywhere without you. So you are just going to have to deal with it," he said. Olivia started laughing and sniffling. He started laughing with her too.

"Okay," she said and laughed. "I love you." He was the first man she had ever said those words to.

"I love you too," he said and kissed her. She was so happy that he had come for her. She had not expected it at all. Daya laughed and clapped.

"The pair of you are so odd but adorable," she said with her hand on her heart. Olivia smiled and laid her head on Joseph's shoulder.

"I am so happy," she said.

Epilogue

"I actually miss my father, and even Jacob," Olivia admitted to Joseph. Although she had stayed in contact with them, it was not the same as seeing them. Her head lay on his rock-hard chest. They were both on the settee, lying on their backs and staring at the ceiling.

"I'm surprised to hear you say that," Joseph replied. Olivia smiled. Not too long ago, she couldn't even refer to Sheikh Solomon as her father.

"Don't you miss your family?"

It had been two weeks since Joseph had left his family. Olivia had tried to convince him to return back to Lebanon but she failed completely. Joseph was determined to stay with her.

A loud knock on the door stopped Joseph from answering Olivia.

"Are you expecting someone?" Joseph asked her.

"No," Olivia said, getting up from the settee. She headed over to the front door. It was not a long walk. She had a small apartment.

Olivia gasped when she opened the door. Mrs. Boutros stood before her, finely dressed in expensive clothing and pearls as usual.

"Mrs. Boutros, what are you doing here? How did you even know where to find me?" she asked. Stupid question. Obviously a person with money could hire a private investigator and run a background check on someone like Olivia.

"Hello, Olivia," said Mrs. Boutros.

"Hello." Olivia was confused. Joseph's mother had never greeted her before.

"Is he here?"

Olivia nodded and let her into the house.

"Mother." Joseph rose to his feet. "What are you doing here?"

"I came to get you," she replied as she approached her son.

"Why? Nothing has changed."

She reached out and touched his face. "I don't like the fact you are living out here alone."

"I am not alone," he said curtly.

"You are living a life that you are not used to and it worries me."

"I am fine."

"Your father and I were surprised when you left and did not return," she said. "So we thought it was best to allow you to marry Olivia and still inherit the company as you were meant to."

Joseph raised his eyebrows. Olivia stood in the doorway feeling rather awkward.

"What happens to Hudah?" Joseph asked.

"You have shared custody of the baby," said Mrs. Boutros. She turned and approached Olivia. "I apologize for my behavior towards you. I hope that we can start afresh."

"I… um…" Olivia was shocked by the sudden apology. She never saw it coming.

"I realize that you are not an opportunist."

"No, I truly love your son whether he is rich or poor."

Mrs. Boutros nodded and rubbed Olivia's shoulders. She then turned to face Joseph. "Will you both return with me?" she asked. He walked over to Olivia and took her hand into his.

"Will you come with me?" he asked.

"I'll go wherever you go," she said with a smile. Joseph brought her hand to his lips and pressed a small kiss on it. He wrapped his arms around her and kissed her forehead.

"You can't change your mind."

Olivia giggled. "I won't."

Mrs. Boutros smiled. "We will start planning the wedding as soon as we arrive," she said.

What to read next?

If you liked this book, you will also like *In Love with a Haunted House.* Another interesting book is *The Oil Prince.*

In Love With a Haunted House

The last thing Mallory Clark wants to do is move back home. She has no choice, though, since the company she worked for in Chicago has just downsized her, and everybody else. To make matters worse her fiancé has broken their engagement, and her heart, leaving her hurting and scarred. When her mother tells her that the house she always coveted as a child, the once-famed Gray Oaks Manor, is not only on the market but selling for a song, it seems to Mallory that the best thing she could possibly do would be to put Chicago, and everything and everyone in it, behind her. Arriving back home she runs into gorgeous and mysterious Blake Hunter. Blake is new to town and like her he is interested in buying the crumbling old Victorian on the edge of the historic downtown center, although his reasons are his own. Blake is instantly intrigued by the flame-haired beauty with the fiery temper and the vulnerable expression in her eyes. He can feel the attraction between them and knows it is mutual, but he also knows that the last thing on earth he needs is to get involved with a woman determined to take away a house he has to have.

The Oil Prince

A car drives over a puddle and muddy water splashes Emily, who was just out for a walk, from head to toe. When she sees the car parked at a gas station moments later, she decides to confront the man leaning against it. The handsome man refuses to apologize, and after hearing what Emily thinks about him, watches her leave. The next day, fate plays a joke on Emily when she finds out that the man is her boss's brother and a prince of a Middle Eastern country. Prince Basil often appears in tabloids because of different scandals and in order to tame his temper, his father sends him to work on a project of drilling a methane well in Dallas. If Basil refuses or is unsuccessful, his financial accounts will be blocked and his title of prince will be revoked. Although their characters clash, Emily and Basil fall in love while working together and Basil's heart melts. When the project that can significantly improve his family business hits a major obstacle, Basil proves that love has tremendous power and shows a side of himself that nobody knew existed.

About Kate Goldman

In childhood I observed a huge love between my mother and father and promised myself that one day I would meet a man whom I would fall in love with head over heels. At the age of 16, I wrote my first romance story that was published in a student magazine and was read by my entire neighborhood. I enjoy writing romance stories that readers can turn into captivating imaginary movies where characters fall in love, overcome difficult obstacles, and participate in best adventures of their lives. Most of the time you can find me reading a great fiction book in a cozy armchair, writing a romance story in a hammock near the ocean, or traveling around the world with my beloved husband.

One Last Thing…

If you believe that *The Sheikh's American Daughter* is worth sharing, would you spend a minute to let your friends know about it?

If this book lets them have a great time, they will be enormously grateful to you – as will I.

Kate

www.KateGoldmanBooks.com